Working in Egypt, Lorna had met the fascinating Miles Faversham, and fallen in love with him—as he had with her. Or so she thought at first. But what about the mysterious Anna Orman? What was her hold over Miles? Had Lorna been right to trust him at all?

Books you will enjoy
by ELIZABETH ASHTON

THE JOYOUS ADVENTURE

Somehow Susan had to provide for her two small fatherless children—and it seemed the ideal solution to turn her country home into a restaurant, especially when she managed to get Raoul Sansterre to act as her manager. It should have been such a joyous adventure—if she hadn't managed to fall in love with Raoul, who was destined for another woman . . .

THE GARDEN OF THE GODS

Cass Dakers had rescued Rachel from drowning off the coast of Corfu, taken her into his home, and suggested that they get married so that she would have someone to protect her—and Rachel was already so attracted to him that she was happy to agree. And then the original cause of all her troubles turned up to spoil everything again . . .

RENDEZVOUS IN VENICE

When young Camillo Barsini walked out on Shelagh, his father Cesare offered to marry her instead—and Shelagh was so bruised and bewildered that she married him almost before she realised what she had done. But Cesare was rich, an aristocrat, twenty years older than she was—what on earth had made her imagine that such a marriage would bring her anything but unhappiness?

THE GOLDEN GIRL

Adrian Belmont had transformed Rosamund from a half-hearted amateur to an Olympics class runner—and of course as a result she had fallen in love with him. But he never seemed to see her as a woman—and why should he, since he was going to marry the sophisticated French girl Madeleine Delaney?

MOONLIGHT ON THE NILE

BY

ELIZABETH ASHTON

MILLS & BOON LIMITED
17–19 FOLEY STREET
LONDON W1A 1DR

First published 1979
Australian copyright 1979
Philippine copyright 1979
This edition 1979

© Elizabeth Ashton 1979

ISBN 0 263 73081 6

Set in Linotype Baskerville 11 on 12 pt.

Made and printed in Great Britain by
Richard Clay (The Chaucer Press), Ltd., Bungay, Suffolk

CHAPTER ONE

THE sun poured down out of a white-hot sky upon the Western desert; little gusts of hot wind stirred ripples on the ocean of sand. A scanty growth of scrub and prickly pear divided it from the road, beyond that there was nothing. There is no intermediate area between the fertile lands of the Nile Delta and the desert. On the one side is vegetation, on the other waste. The right-hand side of the road was bordered by trees, eucalyptus, palms and acacias, watered by irrigation which did not extend across its width, interspersed with barren patches, but it had none of the desolation of the sand and rock stretching away to the horizon on the left.

The desert road, one of the several highways from Cairo to Alexandria, was well maintained and carried a steady flow of traffic. Among the numerous cars was a beige-coloured Chevette. The girl who was driving it was alone, and she kept her eyes on the desert. She was watching for a turn off to Sidi Dara, an Arab settlement where she had a message to deliver to its headman. She had been told she could not miss it, a signpost would mark the turning, but she seemed to have come a long way and her head ached from the dust and glare, although she wore dark glasses and a wide straw hat. She passed a woman in black robes who looked as though she might have come from it. She carried on her head, not the biblical urn depicted on postcards, but a plastic shopping bag filled with her purchases, a not unusual sight but one that always amused the girl by its incongruity. She slowed down, thinking to question her, but at that moment caught sight of the post, leaning a little drunkenly over a stony track. Sidi Dara, white letters on black, but she could easily have missed it if she had not kept a sharp lookout. She flicked on her indicator light and waited her chance to break through the stream of traffic. When it came the woman seemed to have disappeared.

She had been told it would be a good road, but it was not. In places it was barely discernible; a recent sandstorm had covered it. But it seemed to have a basically sound foundation, and she pursued her way confidently. The track sloped downwards into a hollow, and a large sand-dune cut her off from sight and sound of the road she had left. She was enfolded in utter silence, expecting every moment that her objective would come into view. She came to a place where the road divided into several branches, and there was no indication which she should follow. She halted in some dismay. She saw a man coming towards her riding a donkey, a grey-bearded individual in the usual djellabah and small turban worn by the fellahin. He was perched on a pad on the donkey's rump, and the beast wore no bridle, only a rope halter. She called to him:

'Which is the road to Sidi Dara?'

He recognised the name, and jerked his head towards the right-hand track. Afterwards she was to wonder if he had deliberately misled her with the object of protecting his village from the intrusion of a foreign tourist. They poured into his country in hordes and were welcomed only for their spending power, and some of the older ones resented the violation of their privacy.

The girl took the route he had indicated and accelerated as fast as she dared. A frown gathered on her smooth broad brow. The village should be in sight by now, and the man must have been coming from it. There was no sign of the palm trees she had been told marked its position. Sidi Dara was not an oasis, but it did possess wells and the trees drew their sustenance from hidden springs. For the first time it occurred to her that she had been rash to embark upon this expedition alone in unknown territory. She had not anticipated that the village would be so isolated, nor the track to it so bad. The afternoon was well advanced and she did not want to be benighted in the desert. She had understood it was only a few kilometres off the main road, but she seemed to have travelled miles.

Then it happened, the car stalled and stopped. Again and again she pressed the starter, tested the ignition and fiddled with the choke. The car would not budge. She was no mechanic—she could not even change a wheel. She got out of the car and raised the bonnet lid, staring helplessly at the machinery within. Sand must have got into the plugs, the magneto, anything; there was sand everywhere. Whatever had happened she was stuck.

She replaced the lid of the bonnet and looked about her. The village must be near and she would have to walk to it to find assistance. Why, surely that must be it over there?—a distant huddle of what might be buildings and a row of palm trees. She set off towards it, her inadequate sandals sinking in the sand. Distances were deceptive in that clear air, and it took her a long time to reach her goal, only to find that what she had taken to be mud houses was only an outcrop of barren rock, and the palm trees a mirage. On the verge of tears of exhaustion, she sank down on a flat stone, only to spring up again as its heat seared through her dress. It might harbour snakes or scorpions, and the thought of such horrors sent her running back into the sand. She must return to the car and wait for someone to come by, and surely someone must pass before long.

Then she paused, bewildered; the car was not in sight and she had lost her sense of direction. Where was it, and where was she? In blind panic she stumbled along what she believed to be the way she had come, only to halt appalled as she realised she was completely lost; she could not discern her footprints, perhaps the breeze had obliterated them or she had missed them.

Then she saw a moving figure coming towards her, a man on a horse. Desperately anxious to attract his attention, she took off her hat and waved it like a flag. The sun poured down upon the unprotected nape of her neck, but she did not heed it. Had the lone rider seen her? He must. She tried to call, but her voice came out in a feeble croak. Exhausted by her walk, the heat and her mounting fears, her strength had gone.

He had seen her, he was galloping towards her, his cloak, burnous or whatever it was streaming behind him like a cloud. An Arab? It was unlikely to be a European. She had always enjoyed novels about the desert, the handsome sheik who carried the lovely heroine to his tent and promptly fell in love with her, but she knew that only happened in romances. The nomads she had seen in the vicinity of Cairo were far from prepossessing.

She felt a twinge of fear. The man might be dangerous. Then she rallied. The promise of a reward would surely persuade him to help her, the natives were all agog to make all they could out of their visitors, if only she could make herself understood.

The horse came nearer, its pace reduced to a steady trot, sending up little clouds of dust from under its hooves, the same dust which seemed to have invaded her throat and eyes. Its rider was enveloped in a white burnous and wore the usual headdress of white cloth, held on by triple cords. They could be bought from street vendors throughout the land for the price of one dollar upwards. Her anxious eyes sought the face it framed, as he came near enough for her to distinguish his features. They would not have disgraced a romantic hero, a clear-cut, aquiline profile, a well shaped mouth, set above a cleft chin, in a brown face, but the eyes which looked at her enquiringly were of a piercing, brilliant blue.

The girl thought she must be dreaming. She swayed where she stood and said the first thing that came into her mind.

'They ought to be black.'

The man swung himself off his horse and spoke to her, to her great relief in English.

'You little fool, put on your hat!'

Then she crumpled up and collapsed at his feet.

She regained her senses some hours later and thought at first she was lying in her own bed in the comfortable Cairo Hilton. Then as she gazed around her, she realised her surroundings were unfamiliar. She was in an austere little tent, with none of the luxurious decorations romance expected in a sheik's palace. There were a few functional pieces of furniture in white enamel, the bed was a narrow camp one, covered by a grey army blanket. It was lit by a storm lantern hanging from the ceiling. There was something heavy on her brow, and putting up her hand she discovered it was a linen handkerchief folded over a piece of ice. Abruptly she sat up, clutching it to her forehead, as recollection returned to her. The message she had not delivered, the stalled car, the desert and the man on the horse with blue eyes that should have been black...and after that? She had fainted, overcome by the heat and fatigue. She had a dim recollection of a ride through the rapidly falling dusk, of being on the horse in front of him, held by a strong sustaining arm, the grip of which had been both comforting and reassuring, though normally she hated to be touched. She did not know where they were going, who he was, but she was in no state to ask questions, and had felt strangely content, as the desert night descended upon them. Before they reached their destination unconsciousness had claimed her again.

The tent flap was pushed open and a man came through it. The girl recognised her rescuer, and

without his Arab appendages of headdress and
flowing robe, he was unmistakably European, his
brown hair smooth and close cut, his bronzed face,
the work of the sun, well shaven. For a few seconds
they stared at each other, presenting an extreme
contrast. The man was all colour, from his sleek
head to his polished riding boots; tanned face, blue
eyes, yellow shirt and cream-coloured riding
breeches. An exotic touch was a red sash about his
slim waist. Tall and broad-shouldered, he exuded
vitality.

The girl was a pallid ghost, her silky hair so pale
a gold it shone almost silver in the lantern's light,
as also did her wide grey eyes. Her skin, far too
delicate to be exposed to the fierce Egyptian sun,
was marble-white, fatigue having banished her
normal rose petal complexion. She had been wearing a white sleeveless dress and a thin jacket, having learned that loose-fitting garments were coolest
in that climate. The men of the fellahin for the
most part still wore djellabahs. Her jacket had been
removed and her arms and neck gleamed like
alabaster with the smooth creaminess of that
mineral. The only colour about her was her delicate
brown eyebrows and the long lashes surrounding
her large eyes. Even her mouth was pale.

The man's scrutiny might have been admiring
or merely irritated; his face was unrevealing. Only
in the vivid blue eyes a spark shone but was instantly extinguished, but whether it was inspired by
pity or some other emotion the girl could not tell.

'So you've come round.' His voice was deep and
pleasant. 'Now perhaps you'll tell me who you are
and how you came to be wandering in the desert.'

The girl touched her forehead with the dripping handkerchief. Her thoughts were whirling. Predominantly she was aware that her companion was one of the most attractive men she had ever met, and there was something in his intent gaze which disturbed her. She looked at his brown muscular arms, exposed by the shortsleeved shirt, and recollected how he had held her closely before him on his horse, and felt her nerves vibrate.

'I'm Lorna Travers,' she said faintly.

'So, Lorna Travers, at least we have a name for the ghost,' he observed. He turned to a cupboard beside him, and she heard the tinkle of ice. 'Here, drink this, Lorna, it will revive you.'

She took the glass from him. It was mineral laced with brandy. She must be looking dreadful, she reflected sadly as she put it to her lips—sand in her hair, her dress soiled, and as he had said wan as a ghost. A pity, because she would have liked to impress him, as she probably could have done had she been looking her best. Without being unduly vain, she knew that many men had admired her pale beauty, but she had never before wanted to attract one as she did this imposing stranger. She must be a bit lightheaded, she thought wryly, to feel such an uncharacteristic impulse, for Lorna Travers was reputed to be aloof and disdainful, and the men whose advances she had repulsed called her an icicle.

She drank, and the fiery liquid coursing down her throat brought a tinge of colour to her cheeks and the lost look faded from her eyes.

'Well?' he asked impatiently as she did not speak.

'I ... I was trying to get to Sidi Dara,' she began.

'Sidi Dara? You were well off course, but surely you couldn't have been trying to walk there?'

His eyes travelled to her slim legs and narrow feet upon which the white sandals were scuffed and stained.

'In those,' he added.

'No, oh no. I had a message to deliver to the headman. I came by car.'

'A car? I didn't see one.'

'It's there somewhere, but when it wouldn't go, I started to walk and I got lost.'

'Not surprising, the desert hereabouts is a maze of cross trails, but were you absolutely crazy to drive alone into such a place? It was the merest chance I happened to spot you, and you'd taken off your hat. You had heat-stroke and you might have... died.'

'I suppose I was rather rash,' she admitted, veiling her eyes from that disturbing blue gaze. 'But I was told it wasn't far off the main road, and my aunt had a migraine which always prostrates her for twenty-four hours. She wanted to send a message to say she was indisposed, so I felt I had to come...'

Her voice trailed away, she still felt weak.

'Very lucid,' he commented sarcastically. 'But why on earth did your aunt, whoever she is, want to send messages to an Arab chief? Ibrahim is a Bedouin, who like many of his kind nowadays has given up his wandering ways to settle, but he's still a bit primitive.'

But Lorna's thoughts had wandered.

'She'll be worrying,' she exclaimed. 'It's quite late at night, isn't it? When I don't come back, she'll be afraid something has happened to me.'

'Well, it has, hasn't it? But I can help you there. We have a field telephone in the camp and I can ring the police and ask them to contact her. If you'll give me your aunt's name and address, they'll inform her.'

'Oh, thank you so much.' She had some doubts about the efficiency of the Egyptian police, but her aunt was well known.

'My aunt is Lady Augusta Clavering,' she went on. 'We're staying at the Cairo Hilton.'

Astonishment, or was it alarm, flitted across his face, which became almost immediately inscrutable.

'Lady Augusta!' he ejaculated. 'The Hilton! I'd no idea I'd rescued a celebrity.' He looked at her contemptuously. 'I suppose you're one of those modern, reckless little idiots, with more money than sense, who'll do anything for a new sensation.' He laughed. 'You certainly got one!'

'Oh, no, no, I'm nothing like that.' She was quick to correct him. Though caused by a misapprehension, his scorn had needled her. She knew the type of idle playgirls he meant and shared his contempt for them. 'Though my mother is Lady Augusta's sister,' a shadow came into her clear eyes, which was always evoked when she remembered her mother's betrayal, as she considered it. 'Actually I'm one of her protégés whom she took pity on, one of her good works,' she laughed a little bitterly. 'I act as her secretary and general dogsbody, and believe me, I work for my living.' A thought occurred to her. 'You've heard of her?'

'Who hasn't, the interfering old ... I beg your pardon. I know she's a philanthropist with her fingers in a great many pies, and she writes articles and gives speeches upon the social problems of the day which she tries to solve in her own peculiar way, only I'm not a great believer in reforms. I maintain we've all got a right to go to hell in our own way. But what's she doing in Egypt? The problems here, I fancy, are beyond her scope.'

Lorna laughed. 'The population is exploding, isn't it? Too many people for the land to support. She's a great advocate of the pill.'

'Well, if she's trying to convert Ibrahim she won't get anywhere. He prizes his sons as proof of his virility, even if he is hard put to it to feed them all, but ...' he looked at Lorna with a frown of perplexity, 'a charming young girl like you shouldn't be mixed up with such subjects.'

Lorna flushed at the gleam of admiration in his eyes. Normally she despised compliments, doubting their sincerity, or suspected there was an ulterior motive behind them. Her pale loveliness had a devastating effect upon the dark men Lady Augusta admitted to her circle in Egypt, with embarrassing results. One ardent wooer had offered her aunt fifty camels for her. Her heart had never been touched. Her parents' broken marriage had left her practically an orphan, for both had married again when she was still in her teens, turning her over to her aunt, who had offered to have her trained to be her secretary. This upheaval in her young life at an impressionable age had made her wary of the greatest of the emotions. So-called love could be very selfish and cause so much suffering to the innocent among which she numbered herself. Her parents had left her without much com-

punction when they thought she could fend for
herself to pursue fulfilment of their passions for
other mates.

This man's concern, slightly old-fashioned, she
thought—wasn't he aware that the modern miss
knew everything?—amused her.

'I only type her manuscripts,' she told him.
'Often I don't take in what it's all about.'

'So I should hope. A young girl's thoughts should
be full of romantic dreams.'

'Which are unlikely to be fulfilled,' she said
tartly, and he raised his level brows. 'And I'm not
all that young. I'm twenty, Mr ... whoever you are,
and disillusioned. Actually Aunt Augusta is here
under doctor's orders. She had some chest trouble
and came away to escape the damp and chill of an
English spring.'

She lay back on the pillow suddenly exhausted.

'I'd be grateful if you'd send that message.'

The tinge of colour had faded from her cheeks,
and her eyelashes lay like dark fans upon their
pallor. The man looked at her with compunction.

'I shouldn't have made you talk while you're
so tired,' he exclaimed. 'I'll send that message to
the Hilton and perhaps some of the boys will
look for your car.' A thought struck him. 'When
did you last eat?'

'An early lunch,' she murmured.

He looked at his watch. 'And it's now past midnight. You need food.'

She moved her head negatively. 'I'm not hungry.'

'You'll feel awful in the morning if you have
nothing. I'll see what can be done.'

Yet he lingered, looking down at her with an

enigmatical expression. She lay on the coarse blanket and pillow like a beautiful corpse, as pale and as still. The bone structure of her face and neck was classically perfect, age could never destroy the loveliness of its lines, and she was fine in every detail, from delicate wrists to shapely ankles. Her silky hair spraying the pillow gleamed where the light touched it with pale fire. She was a northern lily, as out of place here in the desert as a snow-flake on a gridiron. He had met Augusta Clavering long ago, and even then she had been something of a battleaxe, a fierce supporter of women's rights among other bees in her bonnet, as he termed her activities. Unmarried, with a contempt for the opposite sex which suggested an amorous dis-appointment in her youth, what was she doing to this frail, lovely creature who had been given into her care? Disillusioned, Lorna had said, by what? Disillusioned at twenty with all her life be-fore her, barely a woman yet, a girl whom nature intended to bring delight to some man.

But not to him. He had other more important aims which made him impervious to feminine charms, which had been offered to him all too freely. It was long since he had felt for a woman anything but a momentary interest. Being a virile man he took what was necessary, but only when he was sure his intentions would not be misunder-stood. The last thing he wanted was an involve-ment with anyone as innocent and untouched as this delicate girl lying upon his bed. For it was obvious to his experienced eyes that she was un-touched. Some day some fortunate man would wake her to life and love and restore those lost illusions.

He went swiftly out of the tent as if he were fleeing from a menace.

Lorna stirred and sighed, regretful of her weakness. She heard a murmur of voices outside the tent, and her rescuer's clear and loud.

'No, she's not to be disturbed, she's not ill, only exhausted. I suppose that damned Italian cook can rustle up some grub for her.'

Then the sound of a transistor blaring out a pop song, to cease abruptly as if someone had demanded its suppression. It filtered through Lorna's tired brain that though she had been frank with this stranger, he had told her nothing about himself, not even his name. She had been so anxious to explain herself, she had not sought to question him until she became so weary that she did not feel she cared about anything. Apparently she was in some sort of camp, possibly that of a scientific outfit. Or he might even be on safari; though she did not think there was much game so near the towns, he looked like a sportsman. He seemed to know Sidi Dara and its prolific chief, but anyone camped so near the village would have encountered him. He also knew her aunt, or had known her. Did that constitute a reference? Hardly—Lady Augusta's polyglot acquaintances numbered all sorts and conditions, some reprehensible, others worthy.

Intuitively Lorna trusted her rescuer. Although she was in his tent, lying on his bed, she was confident he would not take advantage of her helplessness. He would do as he said, apprise her aunt of her safety, recover the Chevette and tomorrow she would be back in Cairo, performing her not very onerous duties. Lady Augusta was kind in her way to her niece, whom she had taken under her wing, but it was not in her to show affection. She was generous to the world at large, concerning herself with lost causes and social reforms, but it was all impersonal. What had once been an eager, loving heart had atrophied.

Some man had done that to her, Lorna surmised. She was another victim of the love that was so much extolled, love which she hoped she herself would never experience, for it seemed to bring more pain than ecstasy. Perhaps later on, when she was older, she would meet some kindly affectionate man with kindred tastes who would give her the protection for which she secretly yearned and they would lead a placid contented life together. But the heights and depths of passion she had no wish to explore, in fact she was afraid of violent emotion and believed herself immune from it.

Lorna drifted off into uneasy sleep. Again she was riding over the desert enclosed by a man's strong arm, her head upon his breast. There had been starshine above them, the great white stars which lit the desert night and guided the Bedouin upon his wanderings. She had been strangely content, but then she had been lightheaded, ready to credit a fantasy world, peopled by fictitious characters, adoring desert men who loved their captives throughout their length of days.

But the man who had held her had blue eyes instead of liquid black and turned out to be a hard-bitten Englishman who had questioned her as if she were a delinquent, despising her when he suspected she was a useless playgirl, and when he had been convinced he was mistaken, had told her that at her age her mind should be full of romantic dreams, putting her on a level with the soppiest of adolescents. As if the child of divorced parents, who had only stayed together until she was old enough to be abandoned, could harbour sentimental yearnings in an age which became more cynical and self-indulgent every day.

She was aroused from her semi-doze by a touch upon her shoulder. Slowly her long eyelashes rose to meet the now familiar blue gaze, again she repeated her first words to him.

'They should be black.'

'What? You said that before. What should be black?'

'Your eyes,' she said sleepily. 'A desert sheik should have black eyes.'

He laughed with genuine amusement. 'And you said you weren't romantic!' There was a gibe in his voice. 'Did you think when you saw me careering over the desert that you'd met your fate? Sorry to disappoint you, but I'm no sheik, and the horse didn't belong to me. I was exercising it.'

Lorna became fully awake, and saw he had placed a tray on the stand beside the bed. On it were kebabs of lamb, some white bread and a glass of wine. Suddenly she realised that she was extremely hungry and the food smelt appetising.

'Eat,' he bade her, and as she sat up, he placed the tray across her knees, removing the sodden handkerchief from beside her pillow and throwing it into a corner.

'This isn't Italian food,' she remarked, daintily picking at the meat.

'Why should it be? Oh, you must have heard

what I said. We've had to teach Alberto that we like other food besides spaghetti and cheese.'

'Yours must be a very superior outfit to employ a cook,' she remarked. 'I always imagined that men on safari or whatever you're doing cooked their own meat over a camp fire.'

'You're years out of date. There's nothing to burn out here and we use kerosene stoves. Incidentally, I got through to the Hilton and said you'd be returning tomorrow if you were fit.'

'But of course I'll be fit, and I must go.'

'Do you find my company so uncongenial?'

'I didn't mean that.' She thought the question uncalled for. Was he fishing for a compliment? 'I must be causing you a great deal of inconvenience.'

'Not at all, you're very welcome.' But now his tone was conventional.

'I can't be,' she said fretfully. 'A stranger suddenly thrust upon you like this, disrupting your life.' She took a sip of wine.

'You might even do that.' There was a sudden gleam in his eyes. She set down her glass and looked at him severely.

'I don't even know your name.'

'It's Miles Faversham,' he said so firmly that she suspected it was not his real one.

'Then won't you tell me what you're doing here, Mr Faversham? Are you engaged upon some important work?' He looked at her oddly. 'I told you all about me,' she went on, 'but you haven't said a thing about yourself.'

'It'll keep,' he returned evasively, 'and if you've finished, you should go to sleep again.'

'I've slept long enough, and I'll need a little time

to digest this,' she pointed to the tray. 'But if I'm keeping you up?'

'Not at all, I'm often up half the night.'

'Well then? Is it something hush-hush that you don't want to tell me about it?'

'Good God, no! I'm only afraid you'll be disappointed.' He sat down on the camp stool stretching his long legs in front of him, staring at the toe of his boot. 'Prepare yourself for a shock. To the niece of the erudite Lady Augusta our occupation will sound hopelessly frivolous. We're a film unit on location making a picture.'

Lorna was startled; she had never thought of that. He looked such a typical outdoor man, her mind had been running on safaris and prospecting. But perhaps he was engaged upon photographing wild life and native villages. She said feebly:

'Some films are very educational.'

'Not this one.' He looked up at her smiling mockingly, a flash of even white teeth in his brown face. 'This one's one of your good old-fashioned desert melodramas, so you may meet your sheik after all, though only a pseudo one.'

CHAPTER TWO

LORNA had never met anyone connected with the
stage, or any branch of entertainment before. Lady
Augusta Clavering had the greatest contempt for
members of the profession. Actors and actresses,
she declared, were egotistical posturers seeking only
self-advertisement, a prejudiced viewpoint which
had unconsciously influenced her niece. Though
Lorna enjoyed a good play or film, she never felt
any desire to meet those who had created it. She
was moved by the characters as she saw them on
screen and stage and felt that to encounter them
in the flesh destroyed the illusion.

She stared blankly at Miles Faversham's handsome face, the unstudied grace of his supple body,
as if he were a being from another planet, as in a
sense he was. She was disappointed, she had a
childish notion that a man who exploited his personality to amuse the public must be lacking in
manly attributes, but what on earth difference did
it make to her how this man earned his living?
Then seeing that he was looking at her quizzically
as if daring her to express her thoughts, she said
uncertainly:

'I suppose you must be playing the star part in
this epic?'

With faint scorn she emphasised the word epic.

He threw back his head and laughed whole-
heartedly. There was something infectious about

his merriment and she found herself smiling in sympathy.

'What's the joke?'

'That if Mario Brazzini heard you suggest that, he'd have your blood and mine. He's our bright particular star. Possibly you've seen him in operation?' She nodded.

She had seen one of his films. He was an Italian who by virtue of his sexy good looks was famous in two hemispheres. She had not liked him.

'We're a cosmopolitan team,' he went on. 'Our co-star is Rosina Rossetti, she's half Spanish, our director's American, and our producer Welsh. Excelsior Pictures is an Anglo-American organisation.'

Lorna had also seen Rosina Rossetti, a dark volcanic beauty, not, she thought, the right type for a desert romance, for Arab gentlemen were supposed to prefer blondes. She remarked on that.

He shrugged his shoulders. 'She's a box office draw, that's what counts.'

'But you ... you're English, aren't you?'

'A man of no country,' he said quickly.

'But surely everyone has to have a country of origin. You *look* English.'

'Then leave it at that.' He was curt to the point of rudeness.

'Very well, but what part *do* you play in this film? Are you ... what is it they call it? A feature player?'

'Nothing so important. I deputise for Brazzy. Bob, that's our director, engaged me in Alex when he was looking for a stand-in who could ride. Mr Brazzini misled him; his horsemanship is not adequate to what's required of him. Also Bob's chary of risking his expensive bones, a claim for damages might cost the company dear. Then he discovered I'm something of a linguist, I speak Arabic and the local dialect, which talent has proved very useful to him, so I'm more privileged than my status deserves, and I was allowed to provide my own tent.' He glanced round its meagre furnishings. 'An ill-favoured thing, but mine own.'

'Then it's very good of you to give it up to me.'

'I'm delighted to lend it to you,' he said gallantly. 'I couldn't let you muck in with anybody. Actually there are only two other women in the camp, the continuity girl and the wardrobe mistress, they share and grumble at each other all the time. Jess is a beanpole and Mrs Plummer weighs fourteen stone—hardly congenial room-mates for you.'

'No, oh, I am grateful to you. But Miss Rossetti, isn't she here?'

'We hope so, and of course her quarters are strictly for her own use. We plan to start tomorrow as soon as it's light, one day's filming should finish the location scenes, there's only one more sequence to do, but I've a nasty suspicion that our lovely star has sneaked off to Cairo, which means she won't be on set at the scheduled time. Cairo was put out of bounds for that reason. It's not easy to keep this motley collection together, and they're all sick of the desert.'

'I suppose it does get monotonous.' But her thoughts were busy with the man in front of her. He did not seem to accord with his description of himself. He looked too forceful and too assured to be without a regular occupation and he was too well groomed to be a hippy type. He might be a wastrel or a drop-out, a scion of a good family who had disowned him, he had the bearing of a man of breeding, but that was her fertile imagination again. Good families did not bother to disown erring sons nowadays. Young men treated them with contempt and made their own futures. But why of all things had he got himself engaged as a stunt rider? Surely he could find something better to do, unless he was stage-struck and saw it as an opportunity to make a start. But that again seemed out of character. He did not look like an actor.

'Are you photogenic?' she asked, pursuing this line of thought.

'I really don't know. They don't take close-ups of stand-ins, quite the reverse.'

'But you want to be a film actor?'

He gave her a wary look. 'Might do worse.'

'But I thought actors were dedicated people who only lived for their art. You don't sound enthusiastic.'

'That's another of your romantic notions.'

She flushed at his derisive tone, the warm blood running up under her thin skin, giving her a sudden glow. The man drew a long breath and moved restlessly.

'I really don't know anything about film people,' Lorna admitted.

'You haven't missed much.'

She became silent. She was intrigued by this man, but his affairs were no concern of hers and after tonight they would go their several ways, unlikely to meet again. Unconsciously she too sighed.

He said abruptly: 'Your car has been found, a beige Chevette. That right?'

'Oh, good.' She was relieved. It was Lady Augusta's car and she would not have been pleased if it had been lost through her niece's foolhardiness. Also it would facilitate her departure on the morrow. 'Was there anything wrong with it?'

'Only a bit of sand in the works. It's going all right now.'

'I'm very much indebted to you all,' she cried in a burst of gratitude. 'No doubt my aunt will see that you're suitably recompensed.'

His head went up and his blue eyes flashed.

'Recompensed for what? We may be only a gang of actors, but we don't expect payment for rescuing a girl in distress. Did you imagine I ... we would leave you out there to feed the vultures, unless we had an expectation of reward?'

He looked splendid when he was angry, and Lorna's pulses stirred.

'Forgive me,' she said humbly. 'I was tactless. It's the result of living in a country where everyone expects backsheesh for the smallest service. I didn't mean to insult you.' (How came it that a movie extra could be so sensitive?) 'At least accept my eternal gratitude.'

He laughed contemptuously, not completely mollified.

'Genuine gratitude is a rare virtue and certainly never eternal.'

'I express myself badly.' She was nettled by his reception of what was a sincere statement. 'But I'll never forget you saved my life, and perhaps some day I can repay you.'

He looked at her with lazy approbation. 'That's unlikely, though you could make a gesture now.'

His eyes were on her lips. Lorna felt a rising excitement. If he wanted to kiss her she would not object, it was a very small return for all he had done for her, but he seemed to change his mind, for he turned away his head and went on coldly: 'You're exaggerating. Someone else was sure to have found you.' Which seemed to contradict his former statements.

Lorna felt cheated, though she did not usually welcome casual kisses.

'I'm not sure at all, the place seemed quite empty before you appeared.' She recalled how he had come, it had been a dramatic entry into her life. 'You were the star of that episode.'

'The desert sheik ... with blue eyes?' he mocked her gently. 'You must find my quarters a bit of a let-down.' With a sweep of his hand he indicated the bare little tent. 'No Bokhara rugs, or Oriental hangings, no silken divan and leopardskins, the scent of insectide instead of jasmine, and no passionate lover to fall at your feet.'

His eyes went to hers upon the army blanket. Rising from his stool he bent over them. 'You'd be more comfortable without your sandals, wouldn't you?'

He undid the straps and as during the process his fingers touched her flesh, Lorna's nerves tingled; he possessed a strong sexual magnetism, a useful asset in his profession, but fatal to women. He took one of her feet into his hand and gently chafed the high instep. 'Are you cold? It's often chilly at night.'

'No, not at all,' she whispered faintly, disturbed by his touch, which caused a turmoil in her blood. Miles Faversham could succeed by his masculinity if not by his talent, but she hoped he was unaware of how he was affecting her, or was he doing it deliberately to test his power?

He bent his head swiftly as if moved by an uncontrollable impulse and pressed his lips on her foot.

'Don't,' she murmured as a sensual thrill ran through her body. 'I ... I don't like being touched,' (which was not true in his case) 'and I'm sure my feet are dirty.'

'A bit sandy,' he remarked prosaically. He laid her foot down almost reverently, then drew the blanket over her feet as if he wished to conceal them from his sight. He straightened himself and looked down at her with a mocking glint in his eyes.

'Did that do something towards satisfying your romantic yearnings?'

She moved her head impatiently. He was jeering at her.

'I keep telling you I haven't any. I'm not looking for romance, Mr Faversham, but of course it's your job to pander to it. Was that gesture a demonstration of your skill?'

He grinned wickedly.

'Being only a beginner I take every opportunity to improve my technique. Perhaps you wouldn't mind if I went a little further? I'm sure you'd be glad to co-operate, to show your thanks. Stand-ins aren't required for emotional scenes and I would like to be able to impress my director with my expertise when and if I can persuade him to give me a screen test.'

'I would mind very much,' Lorna returned. A

few moments back she would have acquiesced, but
now she was convinced that he was making fun of
her. 'A good-looking man like you won't have any
difficulty in finding girls ready to let you experi-
ment with them.'

'But they're not here and you are.'

'There can't be any urgency, this Mr Bob what-
sit . . .?'

'Hailey,' he told her.

'Won't be arranging screen tests on location and
you said you'd nearly finished here.'

The mischief died out of his face, and his mood
changed.

'So we have, and tomorrow you and I will part.
You've had an unpleasant experience, but you'll
forget it after a week of the Hilton's luxury.'

Lorna smiled wryly. She would appreciate her
comfortable bedroom and mod cons after the primi-
tiveness of her present surroundings, but she spent
a great deal of her time chained to her desk, or
rather Lady Augusta's desk, and was constantly
under her supervision. Tonight she was free and
not accountable to anyone. She did not value comfort for its own sake, only as a compensation for
curtailment of liberty.

'You underrate yourself, Mr Faversham,' she said
softly. 'I shall remember you for a very long time.'

He looked at her sombrely. 'I'd much prefer you
to forget me as quickly as possible. I'm sure your
aunt wouldn't approve of our association.'

His manner had become repressive, there was
no trace of his former flirtatiousness now. Lorna
surmised that the reminder of the coming exodus
had brought back to him the uncertainty of his

own future. She felt curiously loth to let him go out of her life, though there could be no possible rapport between her fastidious self and a man who was a wastrel, as she feared Miles Faversham must be. Why else should he be serving Excelsior Pictures in such a minor capacity when he obviously had the capacity and potential to raise himself to do something more worth while? He said he was a linguist, he spoke like an educated man, he was even polished, nor did he seem greatly enamoured of his present occupation. She was sure her aunt could help him, she had a penchant for good-looking young men, and was always ready to assist lame dogs. She only had to bring about a meeting between them in a way that would not offend his pride, and then she need not lose touch with him. She said eagerly:

'Indeed she's not as narrow-minded as that, and she has a lot of influence ...' Miles raised his eyebrows satirically as if he guessed what she had in mind. Undeterred by his expression, she went on: 'I'm sure she'd be glad of an opportunity to thank you for helping me, and ... and to show her gratitude. When you're back in Cairo if you'd care to call ...'

'Good God, no!' he ejaculated forcibly, then seeing her hurt expression, he added: 'Thank you for the invitation, but Lady Augusta Clavering and the Hilton are not my cup of tea.'

Lorna gave him her most seductive smile. 'Even though I'll be there?'

'That of course is an inducement,' but he said it mechanically. 'Perhaps if I'm in the vicinity I might look in.'

But she knew he meant he never would, and she was piqued. She had meant to give him an excuse to contact her again and through her her aunt, but plainly he did not wish to do so. Perhaps he had found her a nuisance and would be glad to be rid of her, but if that were so, why was he lingering in her ... his tent, and from the expression that had come more than once into his eyes, he did not find her exactly repulsive. In spite of that it seemed she had failed to make any lasting impression on him, and it was the first time that she had been sufficiently attracted by a man to want to do so. Besides, he interested her and she wanted to know more about him. Hitherto she had found that the slightest encouragement on her part had produced almost embarrassingly eager results. Lady Augusta did not keep her in purdah, she even introduced her to 'suitable' young men, but after a few initial courtesies, Lorna had always retreated into her ivory tower, finding them for the most part banal.

While she digested her chagrin, Miles picked up up a spray gun from the top of the cupboard and aimed it at the insects congregating round the lamp.

'Dratted bugs' he exclaimed, and exploded the contents viciously. The winged intruders dispersed, most of them falling to the floor which was sand, except for a small mat by the bed. He swept sand over them, with his foot pressing it down over their grave. There was a violence about his movements as if he were releasing some inner tension. Lorna wrinkled her nose at the pungent smell.

'Not exactly ambergris,' he commented. 'It'll soon fade.'

She had put the tray on the stand and he covered the remnants of her meal with the napkin.

'That's what attracts them,' he explained. Lorna expected him to leave, but though he moved restlessly about the confined space, he seemed unwilling to do so. She had no wish for him to depart, she was wide awake and unlikely to sleep again for some time. She changed her position, turning on her side and drawing up her knees while she sought for a topic likely to detain him. Perhaps what kept him with Excelsior was a secret passion for the leading lady, and he resented any attempt to detach him from her vicinity. Rosina Rossetti was reputed to be a heart-stealer, and not only on the screen. She was a very different type from herself and no doubt compared with her, he found Lorna insipid.

She enquired ingenuously: 'Have you ever acted with Miss Rossetti, Miles?'

'My dear girl, stars don't condescend to stand-ins!' He looked quite shocked. Then he smiled impishly. 'At least not officially. Rosina, like everyone else, uses me.'

'Oh!' So there was something between them, but she did not like the way he put it. Used him? What did that mean? Miles was watching her with a teasing light in his eyes.

'She asked me to hear her lines and we finished up rehearsing her love scenes ... on that bed.'

Lorna made a movement to spring off it as if it had become red hot, but restrained herself as she caught the glint in his eyes. She suspected he was anticipating just such a reaction from her. His amours were nothing to do with her, and he was trying to be provocative.

'Then you won't require any tuition from me,' she said lightly, seeking to maintain an atmosphere of light raillery.

'Perhaps I intended to give the tuition,' he suggested slyly. 'Cure you of your inhibition about being touched.' Then seeing a flash of alarm cross her face, for they were quite alone and she did not know if she could trust him, he added: 'I've only been pulling your leg, Lorna.'

'And in very bad taste,' she said severely. Her face became pensive as she recalled how the actress had appeared on the screen, her passionate mouth and great flashing eyes. Any man would be delighted to play love-scenes with her, which might very quickly turn to reality.

'Rosina Rossetti is very attractive,' she remarked.

'Not my type,' Miles said carelessly, but Lorna did not believe him. He might consider it unwise to be too enthusiastic about the star, considering their relative positions.

'Then you must be very hard to please,' she told him, looking at him a little wistfully. 'Tell me, I've often wondered, when an actor plays a love scene, is he so lost in the part that his partner really does seem to be a woman whom he adores?'

She was imagining those 'rehearsals' with the lovely Rosina here in this tent, and Rosina Rossetti's love scenes were as explicit as the screen permitted.

'Sometimes he hates her guts,' Miles said brutally, and laughed at her shocked expression. 'But all acting is simulation, Lorna, and personal feelings have nothing to do with it. The director tells the actor what to do and he does it to the best of his ability. With repetition, I imagine it can become mechanical. But I'm not an authority, a stunt man has little to do with such scenes. When and if I become a feature player I can answer your question more fully.'

She brightened a little as it occurred to her that she would be able to trace him through his achievements, if he made any. But she was vaguely disappointed by his cynical description, and she asked:

'Surely you can't make an audience feel if you don't feel anything yourself?'

'In Brazzini's case, all he feels is anxiety about whether he's getting his full share of the camera,' Miles told her drily, 'or whether his partner is stealing the scene.'

'I wasn't thinking about him,' Lorna said truthfully.

'He's our nearest example, isn't he?' Miles was openly derisive now. 'You've got a lot to learn about film folk.' He moved towards her and looked down at her with a slow flame kindling in his eyes.

'But I'm not a stuffed shirt like Brazzini, I'd never find it hard to make love to a pretty girl, and I could at this moment embrace you with such ardour that you'd be convinced you were the most desirable woman in the world.'

'Oh, no!' She shrank back on the pillow, dimly aware that all this talk of lovemaking had aroused something with which she felt inadequate to cope. A flush crept over her pale face and she hurriedly buried her face in the coarse linen.

'See, the mere thought of it has excited you,' he mocked her. 'I'm a better actor than I thought I was. Now you tell me something while we're on the subject of amorous reactions ... and lift your

head up, I want to see if you're lying.' Unwillingly
she faced him, wondering what was coming. 'Were
you completely unconscious when I took you on
my horse? Did you feel nothing in my arms?'

Knowing what she had felt, her colour deepened,
turning the lily into the rose. She supposed he
wanted to know because feminine reactions were
what he traded upon. He had looks and charm and
he knew it. He would go far once he got a start,
another Valentino over whose celluloid image hysterical women raved.

She did not answer his question, knowing she
had already done so, without words, and that her
reaction had been what he expected. A fierce resentment woke in her breast. He was conceited,
arrogant, detestable, and yet she could not check the
question which she put to him.

'But you, of course, felt nothing?'

His eyes met hers, challenging grey, sardonic
blue.

'Oh, I wouldn't say that,' he remarked casually,
too casually, mere sop to possibly wounded feelings.
Her resentment grew.

'I'm not the sort of girl who goes crazy over
handsome actors,' she said coolly.

'I didn't suppose you were,' he returned. 'But
though I may never become a famous actor, you
won't always be an icicle. There is fire under your
snow, some day someone will ignite it.'

'It certainly won't be you!' she flashed, stung out
of all restraint.

She had hoped to wound his vanity, but the look
he gave her was mingled sadness and regret.

'I'm afraid you're only too right. That is a privilege I must deny myself.' He glanced at his wrist watch.

'Good heavens, is that the time? I've been talking a lot of nonsense, and you should be asleep.'

'I'm not sleepy, and I found your nonsense very entertaining,' she told him demurely.

He gave a sharp sigh. 'One needs a little diversion at this game. If it's any consolation to you I've much enjoyed our ... er ... debate.'

It wasn't. She felt he had found her näiveté and ignorance funny and she was used to her male acquaintances treating her with respect. What had started it all? A vague jealousy of Rosina Rossetti? But that was quite absurd. But he was giving her a chance to save her dignity, she said coolly:

'Then we've mutually entertained each other, but I'm afraid I've kept you up. You said you had an early start.'

'I shouldn't have gone to bed anyhow, I'm a night bird,' he told her. 'And you needn't get up in the morning if you want to lie in. I'll see if old Plum can find you a nightdress, and bring you some water to wash in—I'm afraid I can't offer a bath.' He hesitated, looking slightly embarrassed. 'There's an Elsan closet to your right outside, and here's a torch.' He laid it on the bed. 'Look out for scorpions.'

Her resentment died away. He was being very kind and considerate.

'Thank you, but do you have to wait upon me yourself? I mean, aren't there any camp servants?'

'Don't I do it efficiently?' he grinned. 'I wouldn't trust anyone else.' He took the tray and went out of the tent.

Lorna slid off the bed, finding when she was on her feet that she was much more shaky than she had anticipated. She thrust her feet into her sandals without fastening them, took the torch and pushed aside the flap of the tent. The camp was in a hollow between rocky outcrops and banks of sand. Lights were spotted about it like glow-worms, but Miles' tent was set at a little distance from the others. An occasional burst of laughter and the distant thrum of some musical instrument showed that not everyone was asleep. The row of picketed horses stamped and rattled their chains.

Above her was the vast canopy of the sky spangled with stars, the same stars that had watched the troop movements in the desert war, and shone upon much earlier strife and seen the rise and fall of ancient civilisations. Egypt was a very old land and as yet she had had little opportunity to view the monuments which were all that survived of its greatness. That was something she must make time to do in the near future. It was a pity Miles' company was not engaged upon something more in that line than the outworn theme of the Sheik. He would make an imposing Pharaoh.

Lorna performed her errand with some trepidation, but she saw no scorpions. She had returned to the tent and was sitting on the bed, when Miles returned carrying a plastic bowl, a can of warm water, towel, soap, and a nylon nightdress. He dropped the gown and towel beside her and placed the bowl on the stool. Unlocking a suitcase which he drew from under the bed, he took out a kaftan and a pair of embroidered mules.

'That will do for a robe,' he told her. 'The slippers will be much too large, but they'll serve if there's an alarm in the night.'

'Is there likely to be one?'

'No, but anything can happen out here. Got all you want?'

'I'm sure I have.' There were several things she could mention, including a brush and comb, but she did not want to trouble him, who had done his best for her. As an afterthought he did take a small comb out of his pocket and handed it to her with a wry smile.

'It's clean.'

'I ... Oh, thank you so much for everything.'

'More gratitude? You're running up quite a big bill, you know.'

On impulse she held up her face. 'Would you like to take something on account?'

He looked startled. Then a flame leaped into his eyes. Murmuring, 'Since you're so generous, why not?' he drew her up into his arms, and his lips closed over hers. The kiss was gentle at first but deepened in intensity. Lorna felt her blood leap in response, something she had never experienced before. The ice was melting, but before she was nearly satisfied, he pushed her roughly back on to the bed.

'You mustn't encourage me in such folly,' he said harshly. She looked up in mute reproach, but he had turned his back.

'Alberto will look out for you in the morning, and give you some breakfast,' he said jerkily. 'He'll show you where your car is parked. You'll find the track to the camp quite easy to follow, so you won't get lost again, but don't leave late, it's quite a long way.'

'Where will you be?'

'Out on the set. As I said, we leave at first light.'

'Then I shan't see you again?' she asked dully.

'I'm afraid not. So this is goodnight, and goodbye.'

She tried again to thank him, but he cut her short.

'My privilege, and you've paid your due.' He touched his lips. 'Sleep well.'

He was gone. Lorna stared round the tent feeling bereft.

CHAPTER THREE

LORNA fell asleep immediately and woke while it was still dark. Sounds of activity outside proclaimed that the dawn was not far off, and with a feeling of flatness, she recalled that Miles would be about to leave. It had been a strange encounter, they were complete strangers and yet their talk had been intimate, and had ended with a kiss which she had invited him to give. Unprecedented behaviour! She rubbed her mouth reflectively. Perhaps it was as well that she would not see him again; she had no wish to become involved with a movie actor, they were by all accounts most unreliable people. And yet wasn't she missing something by being too circumspect? Miles Faversham had stirred feelings deep within her which she had not known existed, and for the first time she began to realise what it meant to be a woman, but he had gone, so she would have no chance to start an affair with him even if she wanted one. Of course she didn't, she told herself severely; it was merely that the unusual circumstances had roused her curiosity, not only about him, but about herself.

The sudden daylight brought a stout little man with a black moustache scurrying into the tent with a can of hot water and a cup of tea.

'*Buon giorno, signorina*,' he greeter her, beaming. '*Una tazza di tè*.' He placed it on the stand, then pinned back the tent flap to admit light and air. He turned out the lamp, which had been burning all night—Lorna had not fancied being in the dark, nor had she known how to manipulate it. He disposed of the water in the bowl by the simple expedient of throwing it out of the tent, and wiped it with the skirt of the apron which he was wearing. He set it back on the stool with the can beside it. This character must be Alberto, but he had no English beyond a word or two, nor did she know any Italian. He seemed in a great excitement about something, exclaiming: '*L'incidente, la disgrazia, cattivo, cattivo!*' but she could not make out what had happened. Then he pointed outside, said, '*Prima colazione,*' and withdrew.

I suppose that meant breakfast is ready, Lorna thought as she performed her ablutions as well as she could. She put on her white dress, deploring its limp appearance, but she had no other, and did what she could with her hair, using Miles' comb. It needed a shampoo to rid it of sand, but in spite of that, it curled becomingly about her face, shaped like a shining bell to fall short of her white nape. Then she went outside.

To her surprise the camp was still full of people. A camera crew dressed only in shorts sprawled under a huge umbrella, playing cards. Arabs or Egyptians, they were synonymous to her, were grooming their horses. Alberto bobbed up, apparently having been on the watch for her, and conducted her to a large marquee, the sides of which had been rolled up to admit light and air. Large trestle tables ran down the middle of it, covered by a white cloth. At the far end of it a group of men were talking and smoking over coffee. At that nearest to her a single place was laid with rolls, butter and coffee percolating. Alberto indicated she should sit there and vanished.

Feeling shy, Lorna sat down, but none of the group of men took the slightest notice of her. She poured out a cup of coffee and ventured to look towards them. To her surprise she saw one of them was Miles, but he was standing behind them taking no part in what appeared to be a heated argument. He was casually dressed in shorts and a singlet, but he was shaved, which was more than most of the others were. The dark man in an oriental robe with a stubbly chin must be Mario Brazzini, and the one to whom they were all deferring was probably Bob Hailey. He was a short, stout man with heavy jowls, and a straw hat was perched precariously on the back of his bald head.

Miles looked round and saw her, he raised a hand in greeting and strolled towards her.

'So I'm still here after all,' he remarked. 'Unfortunately we've had a setback. Miss Rossetti has had an accident and has broken her leg.'

'Oh, I'm sorry.' Lorna noticed he did not seem to be very concerned about the lady. 'How did it happen?'

He shrugged his shoulders. 'You know what Cairo traffic is. Bob's furious because she was absent without leave, and as her understudy is down with fever he felt she should have been especially careful. The problem is, do we call it a day and strike camp, or do we try to find someone to act as her stand-in, which means a long delay before we contact someone suitable. Every moment we're stuck here doing nothing is expensive, and we're behind schedule into the bargain.'

'There seems to be a difference of opinion,' Lorna observed, as Mario Brazzini waved an excited fist in Bob's face.

'Oh, Brazzini's all for getting back to the flesh-pots, but Bob's waiting to hear from the producer. It's Evans who should decide, he's responsible for the budget, but believing the last sequence was practically in the can, he too went off last night.'

Mario turned from Bob with a disgusted shrug of his shoulders, and stood up. Seeing her, he came to join Miles.

'So you are the lovely *signorina* Faversham rescued in the desert,' he said, his bold eyes appraising her face and figure. 'So romantic, was it not?'

Lorna began to feel that if anyone mentioned romance again she would scream.

'His appearance was most opportune,' she said stiffly.

Mario leered. 'And then he share his tent with you.'

'Oh no!' She glanced appealingly at Miles.

'Certainly not,' he said emphatically. 'I slept in the open as I often do.'

'Oh, Miles!' Lorna was dismayed. 'Did you have to do that?'

'As he says, he often does,' Mario was sneering. 'And native girls come and whisper in his ear.'

'Be careful!' Miles looked dangerous. 'You know that's a lie.' Then he laughed. 'The only people who come and whisper in my ear are disgruntled horsemen with a grievance. It's a chance to get me alone. Perhaps Mr Brazzini is shortsighted and mistook their djellabahs for a woman's robes.'

'There's nothing wrong with my eyesight,' Mario

said huffily. 'Except that I see more than you want me to, and of course no one can manage the extras like you do, the camp would disintegrate without you.'

Mario's manner was deliberately offensive, obviously there was no love lost between the two men, and Lorna was relieved when Bob Hailey came to join them.

'So you're the chick Miles brought in,' he observed. 'How do,' he extended a large flabby hand which Lorna shook finding it had an unexpectedly powerful grip.

'I'm so grateful,' she began, but saw he was not listening. A tall angular girl had come into the tent and he was looking at her eagerly. It was Jess the continuity girl who also acted as messenger for him.

'Well, did you get him?' he barked.

She shook her head. 'No one knows where he can be contacted.'

Bob muttered an expletive and scratched his head under his hat.

'Leaving me holding the baby,' he complained. 'Now whatever I do will be wrong. Jess darling, if only you'd been a head shorter you might have saved my bacon.'

The girl looked alarmed. 'Oh no, Mr Hailey, I can't ride. And I'm dead scared of horses.'

'Don't know head from tail, do you?' he said glumly. 'Anyway, you're all the wrong shape.' He turned to Miles. 'Just a day's work to finish,' he mourned. 'If only that damned woman had waited to bust her leg until tomorrow!'

Lorna felt sorry for Rosina Rossetti, whose pre-

dicament won no sympathy. All they were thinking about was the delay to production. But if all
they wanted was a girl . . .

'You want someone to stand in for Miss Rossetti?'
she asked.

'I sure do. Only for the long shots, she can do
the close-up with her leg in plaster in the studio,
and I want that girl now.'

'Then would I do?' Lorna asked diffidently.
These people had been very good to her, especially
Miles, and she would be glad to do something to
repay them. 'I can ride.'

'You?' Bob's eyes ran over her critically. 'Sure,
you're about the right size and shape. Lady,' his
face broke into an unexpectedly charming smile,
'I'd say you were an angel sent straight from
heaven to save poor old Bob!'

'It's quite impossible,' Miles broke in emphatically. 'Miss Travers is Lady Augusta Clavering's
niece, if she did such a thing you might get booted
out of the country.'

'Auntie needn't know,' Bob pointed out. 'Tain't
as if her name'll figure in the credits—anyway,
most of you don't use your baptismal names. Our
Rosie wasn't born Rossetti.'

While he spoke he was staring at Lorna as if
assessing her possibilities. 'Put you in a black wig
and you could pass for her in the middle distance.'

'Bob,' Miles' voice was stern, 'I won't permit it.
Miss Travers is suffering from heat-stroke, and to
keep her all day in the sun might be fatal.'

'But I'm feeling quite all right now,' Lorna
assured him, wondering why he was so against her
wish to help them.

'You don't know what you're in for ...' he began.

'And you mind your own business, Miles,' Bob cut in. 'You're getting too big for your boots. It's me what's the boss man here. Doc can have a look at her and maybe give her an injection. You don't think I'm going to pass up a God-given chance like this because you think she's too good for us? You're willing, ain't you, love, and that's all that matters.'

Miles made one last attempt. 'I'm not being prejudiced, but Miss Travers is quite unused to this sort of thing, and her aunt is expecting her back today.'

'Oh, Aunt Augusta won't mind,' Lorna declared. 'She'll be pleased that I was able to help you out when I owe you so much.'

She wondered why Miles was so against her doing what seemed to her quite a small thing to prove her gratitude.

Mario, who had been ogling her, now said:

'D'ye know, Bob, I think I could manage this sequence if you give me a quiet horse; after all, I am the star and I could probably help her.'

Miles gave him a contemptuous look. 'You'd fall off, Brazzy, before you got near her.'

Mario ruffled like an angry cock. 'You're impudent! And my name's Brazzini, not Brazzy. *Mr* Brazzini to you.'

Miles seemed about to retort, but Bob intervened.

'Watch it, Miles,' he said warningly, then to Mario: 'This scene needs ... er ... equestrian skill, Mr Brazzini, and that's what we've engaged Miles to provide.' He smiled at Lorna. 'The whole company will be grateful to you.'

'Eternally grateful,' Miles jeered. He drew Lorna

aside. 'Don't do it, they've no right to ask you.'

'They've every right,' Lorna returned with spirit. 'You know I'm deeply obligated to you all. What's biting you, Miles? Isn't it to your advantage too if they finish today?'

Bob cut in: 'Hey, don't you try to persuade her to back out!' He waved his arm towards the crowd outside. 'Look at that pack, eating money every moment they're idle. Let's get going.'

'Lorna, you don't know what you're in for,' Miles whispered.

'Oh, I'm tougher than I look,' she assured him, 'and I've promised.'

He gave her a long look. 'On your head be it,' he told her.

But now Lorna had a sudden qualm. She turned to Bob.

'You do realise I've never acted in my life?' she asked him.

'You don't have to act,' Bob told her. 'Just let yourself be mauled a bit when you get collared. You see you've run away from the Sheik, but he recaptures you. That's the bit we're going to do. Much what happened yesterday, I imagine.'

'Only I didn't maul her,' Miles protested. 'And I won't now.'

'What a lost opportunity,' Mario sneered.

'Break it up,' Bob commanded. 'Miles, you'll do what you're paid to do. This desert sun is making you all insubordinate.'

The whole camp seemed to come alive. Cameramen loaded their cameras on to trolleys. Horses were saddled, jeeps were dashing about collecting this and that. A procession started to move out of the hollow to a flatter space beyond it where the action was to take place.

Mrs Plummer provided Lorna with a shirt, breeches and boots, and the black wig. Since they would all be distant shots, no make-up was necessary except hair and beards for some of the men. Bob came to look Lorna over, and nodded with satisfaction.

'Yep, Rosie's clothes fit you all right. Wig doesn't do much for you, but we have to disguise the colour of your hair. Come with me in the jeep, the horses have gone on ahead.'

During the short journey, she asked:

'I don't want to sound critical, but isn't your story line rather old hat, Mr Hailey?'

'Call me Bob, darling. Oh, the theme's dated, of course, but it's due for a revival and it always appeals to females. There's a new generation come along who haven't heard of the Sheik of Araby, and it's a grand vehicle for Mario and Rosie. Their names draw.'

She hoped for the company's sake he was right. She did not see Miles until they reached the scene of operations. He looked magnificent in Arab dress, embroidered shirt, loose kaftan, becoming head-dress, leather boots and jewelled-glass-belt. Since the drapery about his head and neck concealed part of his face she supposed he could be taken for Mario similarly clad. An Egyptian held the big black horse he was to ride. He in his turn scrutinised her appearance.

'I hate to see your lovely hair obliterated by that wig.'

'It doesn't matter, it's still there underneath, but

it's a bit hot. Miles, I still don't understand why you don't want me to do this.'

'I don't want you cheapened,' he said between his teeth.

'But I shan't be, it's only play-acting.'

'Exactly. Lorna, you do realise I shall have to be a bit rough with you? I'm sorry about that, but we have to appear convincing.'

'Naturally, and unfortunately I do bruise rather easily,' she said, laughing. 'So be as gentle as you can.'

He gave her a dark look and said nothing. Actually it seemed extraordinary to her that they should be deputising for the two main characters in the film. He had said acting was fake, and this seemed the ultimate pretence. Also it seemed odd that scenes could be played out of context. Without giving any thought to the matter she had supposed that a film like a play began at the beginning and ended at the end. Now she had learned that scenes located on the same set were often shot all together regardless of sequence. Many of the interior scenes of the present production were already in the can. Nor had she any idea of the intricacies of cutting and joining. Close-ups of Rosina looking terrified could be interposed between the shots of Lorna running.

When Bob explained the action to her she was rather scared. Her horse would be shot beneath her by her ruthless pursuer. She must run, and when caught and thrown across his saddle she must struggle and fight until she was subdued by his superior strength.

'Make it look good,' the director told her. 'We can't afford a lot of retakes.'

The shooting sequence was soon completed; it was a clever piece of camouflage—Lorna seen galloping, lashing the poor beast as she viewed her pursuer over her shoulder (close-up of Rosina to be inserted here). Then the sheik's levelled gun, and then the horse stretched on the sand (the animal was very well trained) and Lorna stumbling away from it.

What followed was much more difficult. Miles, riding her down, had to stoop and haul her up across the pommel of his saddle, and they had to do it a number of times before Bob was satisfied with it. Miles was not gentle and Lorna felt she was one mass of bruises. Having been got on the horse she had to fight him; the sequence was without speech. She felt bewildered and helpless. Miles seemed like a fierce relentless stranger and even his face looked unfamiliar.

It was no mean feat to control a galloping horse and subdue a girl struggling in his arms but he was equal to it, and anxious to get it finished with. Of necessity he was rough.

'For God's sake fight him!' Bob bawled at her through his megaphone. 'You're furious that he's killed your horse, desperate because he's got you again, but you look like a Christian martyr meekly submitting to the lions.'

'Call it a day!' Miles shouted back. 'She's all in.' Lorna lay limp in his arms as the horse curvetted and pranced.

Mario had come out to see how his impersonator was progressing. He stood beside Bob, who did not

want him but feared to offend him, cool and im-
maculate in a white suit, having now shaved.

'You're wasting time,' he said to the director.
'The girl's like a wooden doll, and though he can
ride he isn't an actor.'

His words were not audible to the two on the
horse, but his attitude was expressive.

'We'll have one more go,' Bob decided. He
shouted through the megaphone: 'Go on, you two,
give it all you've got!'

Mario's insolent bearing had stung Miles. His
grip of Lorna's unresponsive body tightened. He
bent his face over hers, his headcloth veiling both
of them, as was intended.

'Come on, you little icicle,' he muttered through
gritted teeth. 'Show 'em you've got some red blood
in that delightful body of yours!'

His mouth came down on hers, hard and com-
pelling. Lorna's heart seemed to stop and then began
to race. As when he had kissed her before, some
primitive urge woke and fire burned in her veins,
her soft mouth parted under the pressure of his
lips, then she remembered he was only acting and
out there Mario and Bob were watching. She felt
outraged that he dared to so exploit her, and a
wave of fury overwhelmed her. Never before had
she felt such rage. She struck at his face with her
free hand, only to be instantly quelled. In wild
revolt against this assault upon her senses, the violation of her pride and modesty, she began to struggle,
resisting with all the frenzy of blind rage. Lorna
was the granddaughter of an earl and had all the
fighting spirit of a race of warriors. Sensitive and
shy where her emotions were concerned as she was,

her initiation into passion should have been an intensely private thing, and it was being debased at the command of a mountebank with a megaphone. She could have killed Miles if any means had been within her reach.

Slowly he subdued her, giving the cameras time to register her subjugation, and as a final protest she sank her sharp white teeth into his wrist. He muttered a startled oath and wrenched it away. Then, as the script demanded, he smothered her in the enveloping folds of his burnous, wheeled the excited horse and galloped away.

When out of the camera's range, he checked the animal's pace to a trot and then a walk. Relaxing his close hold of her, he pushed the heavy folds of cloth back from her face.

'Come up and breathe,' he bade her.

He turned back towards the knot of men, and she saw bloodstains upon the sleeve of his shirt. The sight gave her a faint satisfaction, and Miles grinned.

'You did rather overdo it,' he remarked. 'But Bob will be pleased.'

She had lost her dignity and offended her breeding to please a common little movie magnate.

'Let me down,' she said tonelessly, wanting only to be free from his clasp.

'All in good time. You don't want to walk back, do you?' His voice changed. 'I did warn you.'

She drooped her head. 'I didn't understand ... didn't realise ...'

But it would not have mattered if he did not affect her so powerfully physically that she lost all self-restraint in his arms. Even now she was painfully aware of his closeness. That she had not bargained for, and her body's response humiliated her, especially as he, his act performed, seemed to be blandly indifferent to her surging emotions.

'Well done!' Bob came up to them beaming as Miles brought the sweating horse to a standstill, and gently eased Lorna to the ground. 'Lady, you've saved the day for us. We'll be . . .'

'Eternally grateful,' Miles finished for him satirically.

Days of heat and discomfort had dissolved all protocol and formality among the team.

Bob turned to Mario, who was eyeing Lorna lasciviously.

'You'll have to look to your laurels, my boy, or Miles will eclipse you.'

'A man would have to be made of stone not to respond to such an incentive,' Mario returned. 'I'd have done even better.'

His lewd gaze made Lorna squirm; she sensed he was vicariously reliving the incident with himself in Miles' place. The stand-in had taken this opportunity to enhance his reputation at her expense. Hadn't he told her he wanted an opportunity to impress the director? He had succeeded, but she could not have felt worse if he had stripped her naked before his colleagues, for her response to him had not been acting. She, the fastidious Lorna Travers, had had her emotions recorded as a public spectacle.

She did not realise that the whole short scene would only occupy a few moments of film. That neither she nor Miles could be distinguished from the principals they were representing and of the three of them, the horse was the star turn.

She stood pale and silent, heedless of the congratulations being showered upon her, feeling shamed and soiled. She could not look at Miles. This was what he had meant when he had said he did not want her to be cheapened, but he had not scrupled to wring the utmost sensationalism from the scene to make it convincing. He sat upon the horse, magnificent in his borrowed robes, basking in the approval of his colleagues and the satisfaction of a job well done. Bob was saying:

'We'll call it a day. That last sequence couldn't be improved upon.'

Mario looked peeved. 'It's over-long,' he said judiciously, 'seeing that neither of them were in close-up.'

'That all you know?' Bob was smug and winked at his chief cameraman.

'*Dio mio*, but it'll be obvious ...'

'Not at all. Provided his eyes aren't seen, Miles could pass for you any day, and what we took of the girl was her thrashing limbs and her teeth in his wrist.'

Lorna shuddered with distaste, and glancing up at Miles caught his cynical smile. So their photographic images would be presented to millions of viewers and he was congratulating himself upon his clever technique, while she felt ravished.

He swung himself off the horse with effortless grace and handed the reins to a waiting attendant.

'Well, if there are to be no retakes, I'll take Miss Travers back to camp.'

Retakes? She stared at him in horror. Would they, if they thought it necessary, have put her through all that again?

'She looks tired,' he went on kindly. 'It's been a bit of an ordeal for her.'

'Yes, you do that,' Bob agreed, noticing with anxiety Lorna's extreme pallor. 'Make her rest and give her a cool drink. We'll be paying off the extras this evening, and will be glad of your help with the lingo.'

'I'll be there.'

Mechanically Lorna entered the jeep and sat in silence throughout the short drive. Miles looked at her downcast face, but she looked so utterly withdrawn and aloof that he did not speak to her.

The driver halted within a few yards of his tent, and she sprang out, avoiding the hand he offered to help her.

'Bring us a couple of long cool drinks, Mustapha,' he said to the driver, who received the order with alacrity, seeing the chance to obtain one for himself.

Lorna went into the tent, and Miles paused to rid himself of his burnous, belt and headgear, throwing them into the jeep, before he followed her. He had merely done what he had had to do, and the violence of Lorna's reactions had surprised him. He glanced at the handkerchief which he had twisted about his wrist as a temporary bandage with a wry smile. That had not been in the script, and Bob had gained an unexpected bonus, but what a state the girl must have been in to do something so out of character!

CHAPTER FOUR

LORNA was sitting on the camp bed with her clasped hands between her knees in an attitude of utter dejection. Neatly folded on the pillow were her dress and jacket which had been rinsed out by Mrs Plummer. The interior of the tent was dim after the brilliance of the light outside, and the black wig merged with the shadows. Beneath it her face looked startlingly white and her sweat-soaked silk shirt clung to her shoulders and chest, revealing the slight swell of her bosom, except for which she looked like a slim youth in her breeches and boots.

She looked up as Miles came in and seemed to shrink. Still wearing his kaftan, he reminded her of the degradation which she considered she had received at his hands. Wearily she tried to pull the wig from her head, but to avoid any chance of it coming off it had been securely fastened.

'Let me do it.' He sat down beside her, his fingers at her nape, loosening the elastic and spirit gum.

'Leave it alone!' She jerked her head away. His touch had sent a nervous thrill down her spine, and she wanted no more of that.

'But Lorna, you'll tear your skin if you tug at it like that. Much better allow me.'

She made no further protest and he gently eased the wig off her head, dropping it on the floor. He ran his fingers lightly through her flattened hair, which sprang back to life under this combing. She turned her head to look at him and there was a wild expression in her eyes.

'Well, what do you want now?' she demanded. 'Have you come to complete the seduction you've already half performed?'

'My dear girl, the last thing I'd want to do would be to seduce you,' he said quietly, a statement which was no salve to her battered pride, merely emphasising that he did not regard her as a woman, only a puppet whose emotions he had manipulated to produce the desired dramatic effect.

'I warned you I would have to be rough,' he went on, 'but I hope I didn't really hurt you.'

'Oh no, not at all, I'll be black and blue all over,' she declared, but that was not what was needling her. 'That ghastly Brazzini,' she continued, 'gloating all over me—he made me feel naked!'

'He shouldn't have been there,' Miles told her frowning. 'I'm sorry that he offended you. What do you want me to do, call him out?'

'Oh, don't be absurd, and it wasn't only that ...' The tent in spite of being in the shade seemed unbearably hot, and she pressed her hands to her throbbing temples. 'I dislike very much being kissed in public,' she said in a high shrill voice. 'Your zeal was excessive ... did you have to insult me?'

'Do calm down, Lorna,' he urged her patiently. 'What I did was necessary, we were wasting time and money. If my methods were a little drastic I did at least get the response that was needed.' He smiled reminiscently. 'But believe me, I didn't intend to insult you.'

'Well, you did!' she cried stormily, finding his calm irritating to her jangled nerves. She would have preferred him to show irritation, angry justification, or any emotion instead of his cool reasonableness. What annoyed her was that he was showing only too plainly that what to her had been a devastating experience was to him only a matter of ordinary routine. So she supposed he would have behaved when he rehearsed her love scenes with Rosina Rossetti on his bed.

'What do you think I am?' she demanded. 'A cheap little tart to whom you need show no respect?'

He smiled ruefully. 'You won't find much respect in this profession.'

'Then thank God I don't belong to it!'

The arrival of Mustapha carrying two tall tumblers on a small tray interrupted them. Lorna took one of them as he offered it to her, giving the man her sweetest smile.

'Thank you so much, it's good of you to bother.'

'He's paid to bother,' Miles observed as Mustapha went out.

'So you consider there's no need to show him courtesy? How much am I to be paid for the exhibition I've just given you? Or do you think gratitude is sufficient?'

He looked faintly embarrassed.

'The company will give you a handsome present.'

'Thank you, but I wouldn't accept it,' she declared passionately. 'And I hope I never see any of you again.'

'It's very unlikely that you will. Lorna, you're tired and overwrought. Lie down and rest. Tomorrow you'll be back at the Hilton and you can forget you ever met us.'

Oddly enough she found that prospect uninspiring. Nor did she think that she could ever forget Miles. She stared blindly at the ice in her glass. She knew she was being unfair. By agreeing to play that preposterous part she had laid herself open to the outrage he had perpetrated. That he considered it a necessary proceeding to achieve the result required was salt in her wound. An unscrupulous cad, she thought viciously, ignoring the fact that he had tried to dissuade her. He was so cold-blooded about it. If he had been motivated by desire, an ungovernable impulse, she could have forgiven him, but his action had been calculated to obtain the maximum effect and would have been the same whoever the girl he had held was. Hadn't he explained that very fully on the previous night? She felt it as a slur upon her femininity.

'Drink that up,' he advised her gently. 'You must be parched. Then you'll feel better.' He drained his own glassful.

Restraining an impulse to throw the contents of hers into his impassive face, Lorna took a sip and then drank avidly. The cool liquid did refresh her. Miles was looking at her feet.

'Let me take those uncomfortable boots off for you.'

She winced, remembering how he had removed her sandals and kissed her foot. It had been so different then. She had felt the first faint flutter of desire, a delicate unfolding of her femininity, which might have blossomed into something rich and rare, but for the crude violation to which she had been subjected.

Without waiting for her permission, Miles knelt down and drew off her riding boots. Boots and breeches had been considered smarter than jodhpurs, but they were hot. While he was doing it she looked down at his bent brown head which looked so incongruous above his Eastern robes. Again she thought he was wasted as an actor. Then her eyes fell on the handkerchief about his wrist and she flushed miserably.

'I ... I don't know what came over me to make me do that.'

'What? Oh, this, It's nothing. It doesn't hurt.'

'But it hurts me that I could so demean myself. To actually ... bite!'

Lady Augusta Clavering's niece behaving like an alleycat!

He squatted back on his heels regarding her intently, his eyes vividly blue.

'Perhaps it was a touch of *cafard*.'

'*Cafard?*'

'Desert madness.'

She leaped at the excuse he offered which would seem to exonerate her, account also for her heated emotions.

'Perhaps I was a little mad,' she agreed, 'that would explain ... everything.' She smiled mischievously. 'Only then I might have given you hydrophobia.'

Relieved by her change of mood he smiled back at her. 'I don't think there's any danger of that, though you've marked me for all time.'

'Surely it can't leave a permanent scar?'

'Not on my wrist.' His eyes darkened, and his voice deepened. Lorna stiffened. Surely he was not going to flirt with her? She could not bear that. Leaning away from him, she felt her shirt clammy against her back.

'Oh, if only I could have a bath!' she exclaimed.

He sprang up and an expression of compunction crossed his face.

'You poor thing, and I've kept you nattering here. This has all been too much for you. Look, get those clothes off and I'll run you into Cairo at once. It's not all that far, you'll be there by dark. Then you can bathe and sleep in a comfortable bed.'

The suggestion was not as attractive as it should have been.

'You can't,' she said, remembering what Bob had said. 'You've got to superintend the pay-out—besides ...' She paused uncertain what further excuse to offer. She did not feel equal to facing Lady Augusta's probing questions in her present state of mind, but more than that, she found she was reluctant to leave until she had to. She did not want to part from Miles until she must, which was inconsistent with her previous indignation against him, but the realisation that she would never see him again produced a feeling of devastation. But she could not say that to him, but luckily her first remark had the desired effect.

'I'd forgotten that,' he said ruefully. 'I can't let him down, but someone else is sure to be going.'

'No,' she said firmly. 'I'm supposed to be unfit to travel, that's what my aunt was told, wasn't she?

So I'll stay until the morning, if I'm not turning you out of your bed?'

'There'll be plenty of accommodation tonight. Brazzini won't be staying, so I can probably purloin his quarters. If you're really prepared to spend tonight here, I'll see if I can't find something more adequate than that bowl for you to wash in.'

His concern for her comfort broke through the remnants of her resentment, and she exclaimed:

'You're awfully good to me.'

His regard was quizzical. 'I thought I'd insulted you.'

'Oh, let's forget all that,' she shrugged. Then clutching at the shreds of her pride: 'It isn't as if it meant anything to either of us.'

His expression changed, a look she could not interpret came into his eyes and he took a quick step towards her.

'Lorna ...' he began.

What he had been going to say she was never to know, for a high-pitched feminine voice called from outside:

'Are you presentable, Miles? I was told you're changing. Can I come in?'

Miles started as if he had received an electric shock. He threw a guilty look towards Lorna and strode to the entrance to the tent.

'Anna, how nice to see you!' He exclaimed. 'Come right in.'

There was an eager expectancy in his face which Lorna noticed with a little stab, the origin of which she would not admit to herself. Evidently he was very pleased to welcome ... Anna.

The woman breezed into the tent and stopped and stared at Lorna in dismay.

'I thought you were alone.'

'You can see I'm not,' he returned irritably, as if he suspected criticism. This is Lorna Travers. Lorna, Anna Orman.'

Anna Orman was a short, dark, capable-looking woman in her early thirties, about the same age as Miles, Lorna decided. Except for a pair of very fine brown eyes, she was not pretty, her mouth was too thin, her chin too decided, her complexion too sallow. What nationality she was was not apparent. She spoke English perfectly, which was no guide, neither was her name. She wore a well cut safari suit and she had a certain style.

She looked at Lorna suspiciously.

'And what is Miss Travers doing in here?' she asked belligerently.

'It's her tent for the time being. I only came in to bring her a drink,' Miles told her blandly. 'But what are you doing here?'

'I'm acting courier for a party going up to Sidi Dara.' Miles became suddenly alert. 'We saw the film unit in the desert and of course they wanted to see what was going on, especially as someone told them Mario Brazzini was there.'

'So you brought them down to investigate?'

'Well, it's my job to know what's going on,' she said significantly. 'Also it was a chance to see you.'

So Anna had known where to find him, Lorna noted.

'Anna, the sleuth,' said Miles, laughing. He laid his arm across her shoulders. 'Anna is my best girl-friend,' he said to Lorna.

'Oh, get along with you!' A dull flush crept up under her sallow skin. 'This fellow is a shocking flirt, Miss Travers.'

'I can believe it,' Lorna returned lightly, though the sight of the easy familiarity between the pair of them was causing her some discomfort.

'Oh, you've had some, have you?' The brown eyes darted enquiringly to her face.

'I didn't encourage him,' Lorna said demurely.

'You were wise, which is more than he is.' Her tone was admonishing and she looked sternly at Miles, like a reproving schoolmistress. Lorna wondered that he stood for it, but he had assumed an attitude of mock humility.

'I'll endeavour to mend my ways, Anna. But how did our director greet your party? He doesn't care for trespassers.'

'He wasn't exactly enthusiastic, but Mario Brazzini persuaded him it was good publicity. They're all clustering round Mario now like flies at a jampot, and he's preening himself.'

'Peacock!' Miles exclaimed.

'Well, I suppose he's got something to peacock about.' She turned to Lorna. 'You must be the girl I've heard was picked up in the desert. I hope you've quite recovered?'

Lorna thanked her and said she was, but Anna seemed preoccupied. She frowned at Miles.

'Haven't you been making yourself a little conspicuous?'

'In what way?'

'This rescue act. Suppose it gets in the papers?'

'Oh, I hope not,' Lorna cried; she could imagine Lady Augusta's disgust.

'It won't,' Miles said easily. 'I'm the least of little things, and no one's interested in my exploits. Had it been Brazzini now, it would be splashed all over the paper, both English and Egyptian. He'd make sure of that. Besides, I'm leaving tomorrow, my part in this marvellous epic is concluded, and they're all too busy packing up to think of anything else.'

Anna's attention was diverted. 'So you're leaving? Where can I contact you? The usual address?'

'For the time being.'

'Good!' She moved impatiently. 'For heaven's sake get out of that fancy dress. If my clients see you they'll start asking awkward questions.' She put her head on one side, considering. 'Actually you're a lot handsomer than Brazzini is.'

'Flatterer, but he's got what it takes, and I haven't.' His hands were at the fastenings of his kaftan. 'Don't worry, Lorna, I'm fully clad underneath.'

'Shall I go outside?' she asked, embarrassed.

'No need.' He threw the garment on the bed. He was wearing breeches, boots and a shirt.

'Are you and Miss Travers *sharing* the tent?' Anna asked icily, her eyes like brown pebbles.

'Certainly not. It's hers until tomorrow—best we could offer her. I only happened to be making arrangements for her departure when you came along.'

Whether or not this explanation satisfied his 'best girl-friend' Lorna did not know, but Anna was regarding her with a very hostile expression.

'I'll take these along to the wardrobe,' said Miles, gathering up his scattered plumage and Lorna's boots. 'You can tell me all about Sidi Dara as we go.' He turned to Lorna, adding pointedly: 'You were going to have a rest, so we'll leave you in peace.'

'So long, Miss Travers,' Anna forced a smile to her thin lips. 'Hope you feel no ill effects from your adventure. Come along, Miles.'

She linked her arm possessively through his and they went out together leaving Lorna feeling abandoned. They seemed an unlikely couple, but Anna evidently regarded Miles as her property. And Miles? It was often remarked that good-looking men seemed to marry plain women. Perhaps they grew weary of pursuit by the other sort and found the homely ones less exacting. He had called Anna his 'best girl-friend' . . . Oh, bother Miles, Lorna thought crossly, I'm becoming obsessed with him, and of course he'll forget all about the bath.

But there she wronged him. In a very short while Mustapha and Alberto appeared with a zinc bath of ancient vintage and several cans of water. Beaming, they filled it for her, Alberto conveying by expressive gestures that they would return to empty it when she had finished her ablutions. They retired, unpinning the tent flap, and Lorna stripped off her shirt and tight-fitting breeches with a sigh of relief and a feeling of heartfelt gratitude towards Miles. But she had better be careful how she expressed it, she thought wryly. He might suggest some crazy form of repayment, and her efforts to settle her former debts had already cost her dear, as certain darkening patches on her white body clearly showed.

Then as she splashed in the rather inadequate tub her mind reverted to Anna Orman. She need not worry, Miles would spare no more time for Lorna Travers while she was around. Apparently they had a rendezvous in Cairo since she had mentioned the usual address. They might even be engaged.

Well, that was fortunate, wasn't it? It meant there could be no further involvement between herself and Miles. Lady Augusta Clavering's niece could not go about with an out-of-work actor, nor had Miles indicated that he wished to see her again. He definitely expected that tomorrow he would see the last of her, and tomorrow she would be back at the Hilton, resuming her duties, and Miles a thing of the past.

She dressed herself in her own clothes, and found her dress had not been very efficiently washed, but at least it was fresh. The two men came to remove the bath, but she no longer felt like resting. She went outside where signs of departure were already in evidence, the string of horses had already gone. But Anna's tourists were still there, she saw the motor coach parked like a modern monster on the fringe of the desert, and its occupants like a swarm of bees buzzing round Mario's white-clad figure. He would be dispensing autographs, she guessed, and her lip curled contemptuously. Was that what Miles wanted? The adulation of a crowd of undiscriminating fans? Somehow it did not seem in character. She wondered if Anna was helping Miles with the pay-out since there was no sign of either of them, and in the clear air every detail was discernible.

The sun was low on the horizon, sending long violet shadows across the sand. Once it had slipped below the horizon it would become dark, for there was no twilight in that region, though the change from night to day was not as abrupt as on the Equator.

Lorna wandered a little way across the sandy waste, enjoying the peace and solitude. Then she saw them, Anna and Miles talking to a group of fellahin, among whom was the man she had met on the donkey in her abortive effort to reach Sidi Dara. Both seemed able to converse with the natives with the greatest of ease, and she envied their fluency. Perhaps it would be a good idea if she took lessons in the language.

She turned and retraced her steps, hoping they had not seen her; she did not want them to think she had been spying on them.

Alberto came in to light the lamp and brought her some supper at which she picked, not feeling hungry, though she had had only a sandwich at lunch time out on the set. She sat up for a while hoping Miles might come to say goodnight, but he did not appear, though the coach had departed with noisy acceleration and blazing headlights. Then, tired with the day's stress, she went to bed and slept without dreaming until the morning light.

She prepared to leave for Cairo in the cool of the early morning, and to her surprise Miles insisted upon accompanying her.

'I want to be sure you get on the right road and arrive safely at your destination,' he told her.

With her fearful experience of the desert fresh in her mind, Lorna was not sorry to have an escort, and his consideration touched her.

A good night's sleep had done much to restore her to her normal placidity, and she was able to regard the previous day's bizarre happenings with detachment. She had made a thorough fool of herself in more ways than one, and Miles was very forgiving. '*Cafard*', he had suggested in extenuation of her near-hysteria, and *cafard* it must have been, and as soon as she returned to her normal surroundings she would regain her usual serenity.

Feeling very much ashamed of herself, she would have preferred to avoid him, but he met her in the morning to make his offer to accompany her with such casual friendliness that her emotional disturbance of yesterday seemed ridiculous and she was anxious to show him by her own manner, without actually referring to what had occurred, that all was forgiven and forgotten.

She asked him to drive, not liking the desert terrain, and he handled the Chevette with careful competence. Their route took them within sight of Sidi Dara and she realised she had been going in quite the wrong direction when the car stalled.

'They ought to put up signposts,' she suggested.

'Oh, they'd get blown down or taken away by the villagers for firewood. There's very little timber in this country and it makes a pleasant change from camel's dung, their usual fuel.'

'How awful!' she ejaculated.

'It's better than nothing and it doesn't smell when it's dry. The fellahin are terribly poor by our standards. Even my camp bed seems a luxury when I think of them.'

Lorna turned her mind away from the troubles of the poor, which though they distressed her, she could do nothing to alleviate, and brooding upon them helped nobody. She began to think of Lady Augusta, who did contribute useful work on their behalf, and that caused her to wonder what her reception by her aunt was going to be.

'What did she say when she was told I'd got lost?' she asked.

'I've no idea. I didn't send the message. I rather think we only contacted the receptionist.'

If her aunt had received the messages, she had not shown much concern for her niece's welfare, Lorna thought a little bitterly, but then she had been suffering from one of her migraines and would have only just recovered. Lorna had only been absent for two days, though the time seemed so much longer to her. The headman at Sidi Dara would not have received Lady Augusta's apologies for her non-appearance, which he probably did not regret. She would have to put that right upon her return.

As they came into Cairo, she asked tentatively:

'Won't you change your mind and come and see my aunt? I'm sure she would like to thank you for looking after me, and you did say you'd met her.'

'Oh, she won't remember me,' Miles said hastily, 'and if you'll forgive me, I'd prefer to forgo her thanks. I shall be too busy this morning to have time to pay personal calls.'

Lorna was disappointed, she had hoped Lady Augusta would ask him to lunch or dinner, but it seemed he wished to break all connection with her. She wondered if his business was to do with Anna Orman.

When he had said goodbye, Bob had made a

heavy joke to the effect that Miles' women never
stayed long enough to be much use to him. Miles'
women? How many were there? And upon what
terms was he with the lovely Rosina Rossetti? Bob's
parting injunction to him had been to go and see
her and take her flowers, which seemed rather un-
necessary unless he was specially intimate with her,
as Bob would be in Cairo himself later in the day
and Mario had left the night before.

Well, there was one woman who was passing out
of his life, and whom he would not regret, she
thought despondently. She had been nothing but a
nuisance to him, driving him out to sleep in the
desert, and insisting upon playing a part in the film
for which he knew she was inadequate, and then
abusing him when he had had to resort to brutality
to make her performance convincing.

She watched his fine profile wistfully as he con-
centrated upon edging the car through the welter
of traffic, reputed to be the worst in the world,
and as they approached the Nile Hilton, the road
was a solid pack of cars, and yet somehow they
contrived to keep moving. He looked so remote it
was impossible to credit that he was the same man
who in the barbaric garb of a desert chief had held
her and kissed her so fiercely less than twenty-
four hours ago. Nor was her composed self to be
identified with the girl who had first responded and
then resisted so violently. *Cafard*, she thought, and
smiled wryly.

He left her in the hotel forecourt with the most
casual of adieux. Glad to be rid of me, she thought
sourly.

Lady Augusta was in her suite overlooking the

Nile, busy at her writing desk as usual.

'So you're back, thank goodness,' she said without looking up from the pile of mail. 'What a little ninny you were to go and get yourself lost!' She glanced up for a moment, peering at the girl through her horn-rimmed spectacles. 'You don't look too bad, though you'd better go and change your dress and do something to your hair. You look as though you'd slept under a haystack.'

'I'd nothing with me,' Lorna pointed out. 'I didn't anticipate getting lost.'

'And to be found by a film outfit of all things!' Lady Augusta shook her beautifully dressed head. 'I did have some enquiries made to make sure they were genuine and you hadn't been kidnapped or something dramatic. Of course they'd see at once that you were a lady and treat you with respect.'

Lorna suppressed a smile. Lady Augusta's old-fashioned complacency was almost comical. Lady was an obsolete term, though Bob had used it once or twice in addressing herself, but it had not been in the sense her aunt meant. She wished Miles were with her to appreciate the joke as she was sure he would, but she ceased to feel like smiling as she remembered she would never have another opportunity to share jokes with him.

Lady Augusta's attention had returned to her mail.

'Go and have a bath,' she ordered, 'and when you're ready perhaps you'll deal with this lot.'

'Certainly, Aunt Augusta,' Lorna acquiesced, not sure whether to laugh or cry. Her aunt's total lack of interest in what had happened would have been wounding if it had not been so convenient. She had no wish to be interrogated upon her adventures and at least Lady Augusta had been sufficiently concerned to make enquiries about Excelsior Pictures.

Two mornings later when fortunately Lady Augusta was out, Lorna was advised of a personal call. Wondering who on earth it could be as she held on to the receiver, she felt her heart give a lurch, as she recognised Miles' voice.

'How are you, Lorna? Quite recovered?'

'I'm fine,' she murmured, her pulses racing. 'And you?'

'Bored, Lorna, bored and lonely and hoping you'll relieve my ennui.'

'I suppose you're out of work?' she asked.

'I shall be starting a new job, but meanwhile I've too much time on my hands. Listen, I'm doing a little research for a friend in the Egyptian Museum tomorrow afternoon. It's just round the corner from the Nile Hilton. I'll be in the vicinity of old Tut's golden trophies. Will you meet me there?'

'I? Whatever for?' she asked stupidly.

'Well, it's very dull in the museum by oneself,' he said plaintively. 'And I'd like to see your charming face again. It would brighten the rather grim interior.'

Lorna had reconciled herself to never seeing him again, though she had daydreamed that they might meet unexpectedly. She had never imagined that he would actually contact her.

'Well?' He sounded impatient as she did not answer. 'Can you make it or can't you? Or should I ask do you *want* to make it?'

'I'm not a free agent,' she hedged. 'My aunt may

need me. I'll have to ascertain that first.'

Which was not quite true. Her afternoons were her own as her aunt always took a siesta. She knew she would be wise not to meet Miles again. He disturbed her and she was doubtful about his intentions towards her. Had he suggested a dinner, she would have refused at once, but there was something very prosaic about the Egyptian Museum, and it would only be a brief encounter. It might even have a salutary effect. Away from the glamour of the desert surroundings, his big horse and his Eastern robes, she might find that Miles Faversham was only a very ordinary person after all. In which case she would be freed from her obsession with him.

'I'll be there all afternoon and hope that you can make it if only for a little while,' he was telling her. 'Come if you can.'

'But Miles, I wouldn't want you ...'

She realised he had rung off.

CHAPTER FIVE

LORNA cradled the receiver thoughtfully. If Miles really wanted to see her, he had made quite a clever move. She would be haunted by the picture of him alone in those great musty rooms watching for her and disappointed if his vigil proved fruitless. On the other hand he had said he had to go there anyway, so she need not feel guilty if she decided not to turn up. She remained undecided throughout the rest of the day, torn between prudence and her desire to meet Miles, which seemed to increase as the hours passed. She continued to waver during the following morning. Luckily there was not much mail or Lady Augusta might have complained of her lack of concentration.

'I've a lunch party at the British Embassy,' that lady told her, when she had dealt with what letters required immediate attention. 'Our government is watching developments here with some interest— the Peace Treaty, you know. I may pick up some information. Take the rest of the day off and have a good sleep this afternoon. You haven't quite recovered from your desert escapade yet.'

For so her aunt termed her two days' absence. Lorna wondered what she would say if she told her all that had actually happened. Her ladyship was unpredictable. She might be shocked or she might be highly amused.

Lorna's solitary lunch was brought to her in their

suite, which comprised two bedrooms and a sitting room. After she had eaten, she sat by the window gazing at the traffic going up and down the Nile. There were feluccas with their characteristic tall sails, motor launches, barges, even rowing boats. There were also one or two cruise ships conveying tourists upon the long river trip to Luxor and Karnak, places which she had not yet visited and longed to do, though the usual route was by air.

Rest was out of the question, for her mind was fixed upon Miles Faversham waiting in the dim interior of the museum. Finally, compelled by an inner urge which she could not resist, she went into her bedroom, showered in the adjacent bathroom, and exchanged her linen trousers and top for a thin, full dress patterned in delicate pinks, blues and mauves, adding to her ensemble a white crinoline straw hat. The image her glass reflected was fresh, feminine, even girlish and a great contrast to that which Anna Orman had presented when she appeared at the camp. Subconsciously Lorna had selected her outfit with the other woman in mind. Then she left the hotel filled with a far greater feeling of anticipation than the occasion seemed to warrant.

The Egyptian Museum was, as Miles had said, just behind the hotel. Lorna entered its gates and walked through the forecourt, pausing to glance into the stone basin of water within its precincts. Blue lilies floated on the surface of the water, the lotus lilies that figured in so many Ancient Egyptian paintings. They must have been more plentiful in those days, for now they were becoming rare. Lorna had been told they represented the soul. A few papyrus reeds also grew among them, a once wild plant which nowadays only survived when cultivated.

Lorna entered the rather gloomy portals of the big building, bought her ticket and slowly ascended the broad staircase to the rooms above where the Tutankhamen treasure was on display. She had seen it before, so she knew her way. Still half inclined to retrace her steps, she sauntered past the life-sized black and gold figure near the entry, noticing with relief that for once the place was not crowded.

She saw Miles standing by the case containing Anubis, the black jackal god, on his golden chest. Usually represented with an animal's head on a human body, in this carving he was given his natural form. Miles was gazing with absorption at the handsome effigy with its pointed nose and raised ears. He was casually dressed in slacks and a short-sleeved blue shirt laced across his broad chest, displaying the brown column of his throat. His pose was unconsciously graceful as he lounged against the protective bars surrounding the case, but there was nothing effeminate in his bearing, rather he gave the impression of leashed force, similar to the beast on the box.

Lorna's heart lurched at the sight of him and she paused irresolute, half inclined to turn and flee. Then he turned his head and saw her.

'Lorna!' His face lighted up and in a few quick strides he was beside her. 'What a vision of spring-time in this gloomy place. I hardly dared to hope you would come.'

'Well ... er ... I had nothing better to do,' she

returned, fearful that her own face would betray her pleasure. She would hate him to know how much he excited her. 'You don't seem to be very busy.'

He looked at her uncertainly. 'I've made all the notes I need, but I had hoped you would be pleased to see me, even if I am only a diversion to fill an empty afternoon.'

'Oh, I am.' Aimlessly she moved towards the black jackal. Miles was having his usual disturbing effect upon her senses. 'He's lovely, isn't he?' She indicated the statue. 'I like him better than anything else, even the gilded mummy cases. Such clean lines.' She spoke at random, hardly aware of what she was saying.

'Those ancient craftsmen knew their stuff,' Miles observed absently, his eyes fixed upon her face. 'But you've seen him before, surely?'

'And I've seen you before. Both of you improve upon further acquaintance.'

He laughed. 'Do you know that's almost a compliment?'

Laughter caused attractive sun wrinkles to form about his eyes, but he was a good deal older than she was. If he were thirty that made a ten-year gap. Time for quite a lot of living.

'What means the speculative gaze?' he demanded. 'Do I displease you?'

'No. Oh no, I was only thinking you must have seen a great deal more of life than I have, and experience always awes me.'

'Rubbish, what you mean is you were wondering if I'm too old for you. I'm no callow youth, Lorna. I'm over thirty to your twenty, but that doesn't make me Methuselah. An older man is in a more assured position.'

'Usually, but is work in the film industry assured?'

'Oh, that!' He looked at her oddly. I've other resources. I suppose like all women you'd look for security in marriage?'

'All women are not so mercenary,' she declared vehemently. 'If they were they wouldn't make so many mistakes. It's love that leads them to commit such ghastly errors.'

She was thinking of her parents. They, though to an onlooker they were obviously unsuited by temperament and characteristics, had married for love, but it had not lasted. She had overheard too many rows in her childhood not to know that.

'So you consider falling in love is a ghastly error?'

'It sometimes works out,' she admitted, 'but there need to be other ingredients to make a happy marriage. However did we get on to such a subject?' She looked away from him into the dark recesses of the hall. 'Are you thinking of getting married?'

He did not answer at once and Lorna's heart beat anxiously. Suppose he said Miss Orman was his intended? She did not believe they were compatible. Anna's manner was too proprietorial and Miles was not a man to allow himself to be dominated by a woman. She herself would suit him better, she was young enough to be pliable, and she was the type that needed a strong shoulder to lean upon, but she dared not hope he would think of her. Dared not hope? Was she completely crazy? She hardly knew the fellow. If ever there were the components of catastrophe they were here. Happiness could not be built upon blind infatuation, and that was what she must be feeling for Miles. A sort of *cafard*, she thought whimsically.

The man's eyes were fixed upon her averted face, the cameo delicacy of her profile, the fine lines of her throat and neck. In that place which housed the trappings of death, she was youth and life personified. He gave a sharp sigh.

'Most men consider matrimony at some time or other,' he said lightly, 'though not as constantly as women do. But surely you're not one of those girls who view every unattached male they meet through the circle of a wedding ring?'

'Most certainly not. I'd have to know a man very very well before I'd ever think of marrying him;' She paused, looking at him significantly. 'But I wouldn't want to break the circle of another's engagement ring.'

'I haven't exchanged rings with anybody, if that's what's bothering you. What about you?'

She stretched out her slim left hand.

'You see I don't wear a ring.'

'It might be an omission about to be rectified. You're still getting to know your intended very, very well.' A derisive note crept into his voice.

'There isn't one.' She withdrew her hand. 'But I don't suppose it's of any interest to you.'

She tried to speak as casually as he did, but she waited anxiously for his reaction to her leading question.

Again he was silent, apparently absorbed in Anubis. The narrow whites of the jackal's eyes and its white eyebrows gave the beast a slightly sinister expression. Then he said:

'Naturally a man likes to know that the girl he dates is unattached.'

An evasive and unsatisfactory reply, but what had she expected? A declaration? And she hardly considered their meeting in the nature of a date. Feeling their conversation had become too personal, she said brightly:

'How is Miss Rossetti?'

'Progressing favourably, I believe. She's been moved to the Seramis Hotel, next door to yours, and Bob hopes she will soon be well enough to do those close-ups to complete his picture.'

'With a leg in plaster?'

'You don't do close-ups standing on your head. Her upper half will suffice.'

'It's a mystery to me how a film can be manipulated to show a smooth sequence when actually it's been shot piecemeal,' she commented.

'You'll have to ask the cutting room boys about that. I'm not a technician.'

Lorna was not sufficiently interested to want to do that, and Miles had not given her the information for which she had been angling. She would have to be more direct.

'Did you go to see her?' she asked bluntly.

'Good lord, no! Rosina's having the time of her life, surrounded by admirers and buried in fan mail. She only noticed me when there was no one else available.'

'And you don't mind?'

'Why on earth should I mind? Rosina's a vain, selfish little moron. I'd like to have told her to go to hell, but it wasn't expedient to do so, she could have got me sacked.'

That seemed to dispose of Miss Rossetti, but there was still Anna, and Lorna shrank from questioning him about her, for she might not like the answers she received. Apparently they were not engaged, but it might be, as he had put it, an omission about to be rectified.

He appeared to be engrossed in Anubis again, and Lorna was about to tell him she must go, feeling a little nettled, what had the jackal got that she hadn't? When he roused himself to say: 'This isn't exactly a date, wouldn't you prefer a dinner?' thinking of Anna, she looked him straight in the face, as she told him:

'Only if you also are free.'

Under the steady gaze of her grey eyes, his wavered and dropped.

'Unfortunately at the moment, I'm not,' he said curtly.

So it was Anna. Lorna felt as if a cold blast of air had suddenly blown through the museum. Mechanically she turned towards the entry.

'I must be going.'

'Wait a moment.' His hand was on her bare arm. His touch as usual electrified her. She stood quite still, wanting to throw it off, reluctant to free herself.

'It's not a woman,' he told her. 'I have other obligations.'

'I see.' But she didn't. Perhaps the barrier was economic and he had dependents, but that would not bind him in the sense she had meant. It must be another woman and he was not being straight with her. She said lightly:

'I didn't know the film world insisted upon

bachelorhood, though I've heard that it's an advantage to be unattached.'

'It's not that. Look, Lorna, I can't be more explicit, I shouldn't have asked you to meet me, but I couldn't help myself. It's difficult ...' He paused as if considering what more he dare say.

'I'd hate to cause you any difficulty,' she said sweetly, trying to withdraw her arm. 'So we'd better say goodbye.'

His grip of it tightened. 'Now you're offended, I've expressed myself badly.' He looked troubled.

'On the contrary, you've been most explicit.'

'I hope not!' he ejaculated so vehemently that Lorna was startled.

'Please let me go, Mr Faversham,' she pleaded.

'Not like this.'

Then suddenly he changed completely. The worried frown was smoothed from his brow, and he smiled at her sunnily, breaking the tension between them.

'I'm not sure what all this is about,' he said frankly. 'We seem to be wading in Greek tragedy. Surely a man can ask a girl out without committing himself, and you say yourself you'd have to know a guy very well before you'd take him seriously. I enjoy your company, Lorna, and you must like mine or you wouldn't have come here this afternoon. I'd like to get to know you better and take you about a bit—I don't think you get much fun, do you? We could have a pleasant friendship with no strings attached on either side, and I assure you if you come out with me you won't be breaking anyone's heart.'

Lorna felt that she had been making heavy

weather about nothing. What had she been reading into his remarks about marriage? A proposal, which she did not want? She had no friends of her own in Cairo and his offer was very attractive. What if he were on the verge of contracting himself to Anna? He had not done so yet, and in any case an engagement was not a marriage. Friendship without strings attached was exactly what she wanted from him, a chance to get to know *him* better, and enjoy his company, for in it she felt herself waking to new life; for confined to Lady Augusta's service, she felt her youth was passing away in sterile bondage.

'I'd be happy to accept that,' she said.

Strangely enough he looked dissatisfied. He released her arm and thrust his hand into his trouser pocket.

'Even though all you know of me is that I'm an unsuccessful movie actor?'

'You don't seem anxious to tell me any more, but perhaps you will in time,' Lorna said hopefully. 'But I'm sure you'll make good very soon.' She hesitated. 'I ... I suppose you'll be going away before long?'

'Possibly, but I live for today and let tomorrow take care of itself. Haven't you had enough of this gloomy mausoleum? Let's get out into the sunshine. Have you seen the papyrus factory? It's not terribly exciting, but it's a pleasant spot and it's down by the river. It'll be cooler there.'

She had not, and she did not care where they went so long as she was with him.

Actually the factory was situated on a houseboat moored to the shore, and the way to it was through a small garden full of trees with seats set beneath them. Cottages surrounded the small enclosure where climbing clematis grew and geraniums in pots. The paper was made by pressing together horizontal strips of the fibre inside the reeds, and a second layer laid crosswise on top of the first. The strips of fibre looked like white tape. Lorna was not very interested in the manufacturing process. The finished result was a strong fawn-coloured parchment, and pieces were for sale stamped with Egyptian designs.

They sat under the trees and Miles fetched her a cool drink from one of the cottages which sold refreshments. A ginger cat approached them with upraised tail, intent upon making friends. The river was visible between the houseboat and other moored craft, and there were few people about.

'It's very peaceful here,' Lorna observed after they had sat awhile in companionable silence.

'Yes, it's difficult to realise the bustle of the city is just round the corner.' Absently Miles stroked the cat. 'Cats were sacred to the Ancient Egyptians. They had a cat-headed goddess and many mummies of cats have been found.'

'They were a fascinating people. I do so want to go up the Nile and see some of the temples.'

'Haven't you been? Then I'll take you.'

'Oh no. I mean ... I wasn't fishing and I doubt if I could get enough time off.'

'Is your august employer such a tyrant?'

'Not at all, but it's due to her generosity that I'm here at all, so I feel I must defer to her wishes.'

He gave her a sidelong look. 'Such devotion to duty is most commendable and becoming rare.'

for his favours? Her eyes dropped to her hands clasped on her knees.

'Do you think I'm naïve, Miles?'

'I think you're charming.'

Of course he would say something like that, he would consider it ungallant to give her a truthful answer. She stood up reluctantly.

'I must go.'

'I'll put you in a taxi, but first ...' He handed her a cardboard envelope which he had placed on the table when they sat down. 'A little memento of our afternoon.'

'Miles, you mustn't give me presents,' she protested.

'It's only a trifle. Have a look at it.'

It was a sheet of papyrus on which was stamped Anubis on his golden box.

'Miles, it's beautiful! I'll treasure it always.'

'I'd like to have given you something much more valuable,' he declared, 'but I knew you wouldn't take it.'

He looked at her questioningly.

'You're quite right, I couldn't,' she said firmly.

She replaced Anubis in his envelope as he said approvingly:

'Good girl!'

She looked at him provocatively.

'Sometimes I wish I wasn't ... a good girl.'

'Never wish that,' he told her earnestly. 'The other sort are bloodsuckers.'

'I certainly wouldn't want to be that,' she observed, moving towards the entrance.

'You couldn't,' he returned succinctly.

Lorna heard nothing from Miles during the following week. When he left her he had said he would be getting in touch with her, but when she had ventured to ask where he was staying, he had told her he had no permanent address.

'I'm just moving around looking for a suitable job.'

It was unlikely, she thought, that he would find one in Egypt, and weren't there regulations about foreigners working there? Certainly if he decided to continue in films he would have to leave the country, and the fear of his imminent departure hung over her like a cloud. He seemed to delight in clothing himself in mystery, but it never occurred to her to doubt his integrity. Nor was there any doubt about his fascination for her, she was simply living until she heard from him again.

Anubis stood framed upon her dressing table. There was a knowing look in the white-ringed eye, the alertly pricked ear, as if he were watching some distant prey. Anubis presided at the ceremonies for the dead, there is one picture where he is shown weighing human souls. He'd find mine wanting, Lorna thought; instead of taking an interest in my worthy aunt's schemes for the betterment of the deprived, I'm preoccupied solely with that man.

If she had fallen in love it was a state of being which fell far short of the rapture it was supposed to be. All she experienced was an intense restlessness, an inability to concentrate and a longing for his presence, while at the same time dreading he might suspect her feelings if they met again. She doubted her powers of dissimulation where he was concerned. She began to have some sympathy for her school friends' adolescent crushes which she had previously scorned. For that's all I'm suffering from, she assured herself, a long-overdue crush on a man who is actually almost a stranger to me. It'll fade in time as theirs used to do. But those girls had never been embraced and kissed by the objects of their adoration, and her body refused to forget that experience though her mind tried to banish it.

In her dreams she was often in his arms again, waking to the bitter recollection that on his part it had been play-acting.

Lady Augusta remarked upon her absentmindedness.

'Really, I'd think you were in love,' she said, 'if I didn't know you haven't met anyone to fall in love with.' She gave Lorna a sharp glance. 'You haven't, have you?'

Lorna hoped she had not blushed. 'As you say, I haven't met anyone suitable,' she replied demurely.

Her aunt would not consider Miles Faversham suitable, having the greatest contempt for actors and actresses—mountebanks, she called them. Though Lorna worked for Lady Augusta in a dependent position, she was still her sister's child, and her aunt's democratic ideas were not extended to her own family. When Miles had brought her back she might have tolerated him out of gratitude for the service he had done her. But he had refused to meet her and the opportunity had been lost. Lorna was of age and had the right to choose her own companions, but she knew Lady Augusta would make difficulties if she knew who she was meeting. Therefore it was better she did not know about him, especially as he seemed to have forgotten his offer of friendship. She looked disconsolately at the calendar. Was it really only a week since she had met him in the museum?

Then at last he rang her up. Providentially, as on the first occasion, it was when Lady Augusta was out. It crossed her mind that he might be aware of her aunt's movements, but that was unlikely unless he kept a watch on the hotel, which was still more improbable. Yet, after the usual conventional greeting, he said to her:

'Lady Augusta is spending next weekend in Alex, isn't she?'

'Yes, she's been invited by some V.I.P.—but how did you know that?'

'Both she and her host are much publicised people,' he explained. 'It's easy to check their movements. Are you going?'

'I'm not wanted. There'll be plenty of secretarial help available, and I'm glad to be excused. It'll be a very dull conference.'

'Then what does she expect you to do with yourself?'

'Rest,' Lorna told him. 'She insists that I'm still looking peaky, but really I'm perfectly all right.'

'Fit to embark upon a trip up to Luxor?'

'Luxor? But that's impossible!'

'A word that isn't in my vocabulary. I have to go into Upper Egypt to make a business contact and I thought you might like to come along as you want to see the ruins.'

'Like to!' she breathed. 'I ... I'd love to.'

'Then that's settled,' he said blithely. 'We'll

spend Saturday night at a hotel, all exes paid, of course.'

A night at a hotel? What did he think she was, one of those permissive girls who took a weekend with a man in their stride? He was presuming upon the terms of their friendship.

'I'm sorry, I'm afraid it's quite out of the question,' she said frigidly.

'Why ever not? I'll get you back on Sunday night and your aunt won't be returning until Monday, will she?'

'Miles, I couldn't,' her voice quivered. 'I'm not that sort of girl.'

'What's that got to do with it? Oh, I see.' He began to laugh. 'Miss Travers, this is not a seduction act. I'll book separate rooms, of course. Since I have to go I'd like to show you Luxor and Karnak.' He hesitated. 'Actually it was Bob's idea, he felt the company ought to make you some recompense for helping them out, and we hit on this idea of giving you a treat.'

It sounded quite plausible and she began to waver.

'That's awfully kind of him, but I still think it's ... it's ...' she sought for a word that would not offend him, 'unconventional.'

'Oh, come off it! Who bothers about conventions nowadays? Do you want me to engage a duenna?'

Lorna was silent, inclination wrestling with caution.

'You don't trust me?' he asked in a changed voice. 'But you spent two nights in my tent in the desert and that didn't seem to worry you.'

'That was expedient ...' she began.

'So's this. I want you to come. You must learn to snatch your opportunities, my girl, they don't come again. I promise you I'll behave like a gentleman—I always do when I have a lady in my care.'

Lorna went off at a tangent.

'So you've done this trip before ... with a lady?'

'Oh, several times. Do you want a reference from the lady?'

There was laughter in his voice and she knew he was teasing her, but had the lady been Anna?

'I don't think that will be necessary,' she said primly. 'Oh, Miles, I'd love to come, but ... but ...'

'To hell with your buts! Be a devil for once. You won't have much fun alone in the Nile Hilton with me far away.'

The thought of a lonely weekend pining for Miles was not inspiring. A reckless wave swept over her. Let prudence go hang. Those who never ventured never had.

'Thank you so much, I'd love to come, but Miles ...'

'Yes, my darling?'

'I can't come if you call me that.'

'Then I won't, whatever the temptation. Miss Travers, will you accompany me up the Nile? There will be lots of other people to chaperone you, both on the plane and in the hotel.'

'Of course.' She had forgotten that.

'Wear something cool,' he went on. 'It'll be hotter there.'

'Shorts?'

'Um—no. The natives, you understand ... a thin dress would be best.'

'Where do I meet you? At the airport? Please hurry, Aunt Augusta will be coming back.'

They made their arrangements and barely had Miles rung off when Lady Augusta stalked in.

'Who was that?' she demanded.

'Wrong number,' Lorna said glibly. She looked at the handsome, assured woman in her well tailored linen suit and wondered if she dared tell her about the proposed Nile trip. She hated deceiving her, and yet if she vetoed it, it would make her position very difficult, for she was determined to go. She would insist that her free time was her own and it was nobody's business what she did in it, but a blazing row which might easily blow up would spoil all her glad anticipation of the trip. She decided she would tell her aunt about it when she came back, not before she went.

'You're looking a lot better,' Lady Augusta surveyed her critically. 'Got quite a colour. I was thinking perhaps you'd better come with me to Alexandria after all.'

Lorna's heart sank. 'Would I be any use?' she faltered.

'None whatever,' her ladyship told her cheerfully, 'but it'll be a bit dull for you here alone.'

'So it will in Alex, I don't know anybody there.' She gripped her courage firmly. 'As a matter of fact I was thinking of taking one of those air trips up to Luxor, and see something of the temples.' Lady Augusta frowned. 'Lots of people do go on them.'

'Too many,' her aunt declared. 'I loathe public transport myself.' In spite of her democratic principles, Lady Augusta always contrived to travel in one of her friends' boats or planes. 'But if you can put up with a lot of tourists, go by all means. Got enough money?'

'Plenty.' Lorna had not spent much of the generous salary she was paid. 'Thank you, Aunt Augusta.'

The older woman's hard face relaxed into a smile.

'You're a good little soul, Lorna, and quite a help to me. Go on your trip and I hope you enjoy it, but don't over-exert yourself.'

'I promise I won't.' Lorna was relieved, for she had more or less come clean. She had not mentioned Miles, but so far as her aunt was concerned, their meeting could be a coincidence. Anyone could go on a public flight.

CHAPTER SIX

THE modern town of Luxor on the east bank of
the Nile is built on the site of ancient Thebes, the
capital of Egypt three thousand years ago, a city
about six miles square which Homer described as
'Hundred-gated Thebes.' The Pharaohs of the New
Kingdom had vied with each other in the building of magnificent temples, but it was already in
decline when the Assyrians sacked it in 661 B.C.,
and though rebuilt it never recovered its ancient
glory and at the time of Christ had dwindled to a
mere village. Situated on an alluvial plain, nothing is left of the old town, but to the north and
south, the ruins of its temples are still impressive.

On the west bank of the river are the remains
of the City of the Dead, mortuary temples and
tombs. Here also were housed the priests who minis-
tered to the rites for the departed, soldiers who
guarded (ineffectually it seemed) their remains and
the workmen who built the edifices. Owing to
robbery, the later tombs were hidden in the Theban Hills, the famous Valley of the Kings.

Miles and Lorna arrived at midday by plane
from Cairo. They were booked at the Luxor Hotel,
single rooms on different floors. Lorna went first
to register and collect her key at Miles' suggestion.
He was being careful of her reputation. While she
waited for him as he in his turn approached the

reception desk, she saw the clerk hand him a folded note. He read it and frowned. Coming to her, he told her:

'I'm afraid I'll have to leave you after lunch, I have an appointment. As it's very hot you'd better stay in the cool. I'll only be about a couple of hours.'

'Stay indoors?' Lorna looked at him in wide-eyed reproach, 'when there's so much to see and we have so little time here? The heat won't kill me and I can't just sit about indoors.'

She was disappointed that he had to leave her, but he had told her that he had come on business, so she could not expect to have his escort all the time.

He smiled at her eagerness.

'Well then, indefatigable one, I suggest that you take a horse-drawn carriage this afternoon and go to the Temple of Luxor to the south. I'll get a porter to hire one for you— they're quite a feature of the place. The nave of Amenhotep's hall is worth seeing and it won't be too exhausting.'

Amenhotep the Third was the Pharaoh who had built the most impressive buildings in Thebes.

'Tomorrow morning we'll go to Karnak,' Miles went on, 'but tonight ...' he paused tantalisingly, 'I've something very special laid on for this evening.'

'Have you?' She looked at him doubtfully. She did not know his tastes and he might not be partial to ruins. 'Not ... not a night club?' she asked anxiously. 'I really don't appreciate belly-dancing.'

'Nor do I. I'm not enthralled by fleshy women wriggling their avoirdupois. Nor do I think there are any in Luxor. No, I've planned an expedition by moonlight, and there is a moon tonight, which I'm sure you'll enjoy.'

'Oh? Where to?'

'Wait and see.'

Her curiosity aroused, she said: 'But if you told me now I could look forward to it.'

Miles shook his head. 'If you anticipate too much you might be disappointed.'

Over lunch Lorna tried to question him about his business. She knew so little of what he did or intended to do, and all that concerned him was of vital interest to her.

She enquired tentatively: 'Is someone contemplating making a film up here?' For that seemed the most likely reason to have brought him to Luxor.

He gave her a veiled look.

'Not that I know of.' He hesitated, then said frankly: 'As a matter of fact I'm doing a little dealing in antiques and handicrafts.'

'That's a new departure, surely?'

'Not really. I've always been interested in old things and there are still collectors' pieces to be picked up in the bazaars. Then there are native craftsmen who make better things than the usual tourist junk who will sell to me for redistribution.'

'But do you know anything about such trading?' It seemed to her he was embarking upon a risky enterprise.

'I know enough not to be cheated,' he said with a grin. 'I've contacts ready to purchase or to sell. One of them wants to see me this afternoon. The joy of this work is that it gives me a chance to travel about the country.'

'I see.' But she felt his chances were doubtful. Perceiving that he was watching her closely, she laughed and said lightly:

'It's a bit of a descent from being a sheik to a pedlar. Do you travel with a pack on your back?'

'Not exactly. I've ... er ... a depot near here to store the stuff.'

'Is it open to the public?' she asked, thinking that perhaps he might show it to her.

'Not at the moment.' He squashed the idea before she could mention it.

'I wish you every success,' she said conventionally.

'I'm usually successful,' he informed her confidentally. 'In all my undertakings.'

That sounded fine, though he had not progressed very far with his film career, but he had not been serious about that. Lorna was beginning to want much more than the casual friendship that he had offered to her, but there seemed to be little hope of forming a permanent relationship with such a will-o'-the-wisp as he appeared to be.

Miles departed after their meal and Lorna went to find her carriage, feeling with his going as if the sun had been eclipsed. In reality it was shining with intense brilliance. The conveyance was an open four-wheeled vehicle, and the back seat fitted with a hood that could be raised or lowered, with the driver perched up in front. The single horse, Lorna noted with relief, looked well fed.

The temple, dedicated to Amon-re, the God of Thebes, was close to the river, parallel with its banks. The hypostyle hall had at one time been converted into a Christian church.

The great court is surrounded on three sides by

a double row of graceful columns carved to represent papyrus clusters, their capitals the umbels of the papyrus plant in bud. Lorna recalled the factory in Cairo and wished Miles were with her. She stood in the unfinished colonnade of Amenhotep's great hall, overawed by the vast size of the pillars which soared up high above her head. The guide droned on about the New Kingdom, to which period Amenhotep belonged, and the ancient glories of the palaces which had once stood beside the temple, but Lorna's mind had reverted to Miles. Where had he found the wherewithal to start trading? He could not have saved much on a stunt man's wages. True, he had told her he had other resources, and his finances were not her business, but she hoped it was all on the level. Then it occurred to her that Anna might be in it with him, and there was a business connection as well as a sentimental one. That idea, she found, did not please her at all.

She left the great temple as the afternoon waned and drove back to the hotel.

The evening expedition was pure magic. Miles had hired a car and he had arranged with a ferryman to take it and them across the river in a flat-bottomed boat. The moon had risen, flooding the flat land with silvery light. A large expanse round Luxor was flood plain, but at that time of year the river was low and the flats exposed.

The sandy valleys on the western side comprised one vast necropolis. The ancient Egyptians had been much preoccupied with death; they even brought a mummy into their feasts to keep themselves reminded of it. The graveyard of Thebes was a mass of mortuary temples and tombs reach-ing to the Theban hills.

But it was to none of these that Miles took Lorna that night, but through the cultivated land between the desert and the river until they had a clear view of the colossi of Memnon. Then they left the car and walked nearer to them.

Largest and most splendid of all the erections there had been Amenhotep the Third's mortuary temple, but nothing had survived except a few foundation stones and the two great statues which had originally flanked the gateway in front of the temple pylon. Temple and pylon had gone, and they were left like lonely sentinels in the midst of fields. They both represented the Pharaoh him-self and with their crowns on had been nearly seventy feet high; each was hewn from a single block of stone. The crowns had disappeared, and the stone was battered by the passing of the cen-turies. The northern one had been celebrated in classical times as the 'Singing Memnon' because on certain days shortly after sunrise it emitted a curious high note, until during Roman times it was patched up with masonry and never sang again.

In the moonlight the scars inflicted by time and weather were mellowed. The giant figures gazed towards the river, remote and mysterious as they had done for centuries. They were not beautiful, but they had stupendous dignity, an awe-inspiring majesty.

Lorna turned to Miles, her face vivid with pleasure.

'They're wonderful, Miles, and how the moonlight enhances them. I'll never forget tonight, and I can never thank you enough.'

Moolight silvered her bare head, and swathed in the white shawl she had put on because the evening was much cooler than the day she looked like a pale wraith herself, as frail and delicate as the statues were dark and strong. Miles beside her was a grey shadow, in pullover and pants of that colour.

'I could tell you how to do that,' he said in a strangled voice, and she became aware of electricity in the air. He was gazing at her avidly and the bright moonlight showed the glitter in his eyes.

She knew what he wanted and her heart beat so fast she felt she was suffocating. Wild excitement stirred her blood. It was then that she knew he meant everything to her. For her he epitomised glamour and romance, things she had previously despised. But they were not to be despised. They gave to the dull mediocrity of everyday life rainbow hues. This was what her parents had known, and even though their life together had degenerated into bickerings and squabbles they had had their glorious hour in which she had been conceived. For this passion which she felt for Miles she was sure was the real thing, there was a real thing in spite of what the cynics said, and it had crept upon her unawares. In a burst of revelation like sunlight breaking through cloud she knew that she loved Miles with a deep and ineradicable passion.

She swayed towards him, invitation on her lips and love-light in her eyes. She was his, to do with what he would, and she did not care what came afterwards.

His response was swift and fierce, and as his arms

enfolded her she felt a surge of triumph. He felt as she did, and her body seemed to melt into his.

If there were other people in the vicinity, and there probably were—the colossi by moonlight was a famous spectacle—they were not apparent. They seemed to have the whole moonlit scene to themselves. Miles' embrace became close to the point of pain, but Lorna gloried in it. Her lips parted under the pressure of his mouth. His hands moved over her body, subtly caressing her, until he crushed her even closer and his kiss seemed to draw her soul from her body. Fire seemed to course through her veins, her bones turned to jelly as their beings were merged into one.

Then suddenly he changed, she felt his body stiffen and become taut, and almost roughly he pushed her away from him.

'You're driving me crazy,' he said thickly. 'If I'm to continue to be a good boy there must be no more of this.'

'But I love your craziness,' she whispered.

'Stop it, Lorna,' he said harshly, and turned away from her.

She crossed her arms over her breast in a futile effort to quell the wild tumult in her blood. Her attitude was that of the stone Pharaohs who are shown holding the crook and the flail in either hand above their crossed arms. Childishly she asked:

'Do you love me ... a little, Miles?'

'A little!' he exclaimed. Then he seemed to get a grip upon himself. Turning back to her, he said gently:

'Child, don't be misled by the seduction of moonlight and a sexual urge. They have no permanency.'

He straightened his shoulders as if discarding a burden. 'We'd better be getting back.'

He stode away towards the car and she followed meekly, bewildered and chilled by his abrupt change of mood. A sexual urge? Was that all it had been to him? An urge excited by her foolish overture?

The gigantic figures stared indifferently towards the moon which they had seen rise for so many centuries, but for Lorna the enchantment had gone from the evening. They were only ugly masses of stone and the moonlight was harsh and garish. Her heart was hot and sore within her at Miles' rejection, and he had rejected her, for he must have known she was offering him her heart.

When they re-crossed the river, he laughed and joked with the old man who rowed them, speaking in his own tongue, but to Lorna he did not speak. She feared that her behaviour had embarrassed him.

Before entering the hotel, he stopped, and Lorna's heartbeats quickened. Was he going to relent? The shadow from a palm tree obscured his face so that she could not see its expression, but when he spoke his voice was gentle, almost humble.

'Lorna, I would ask you to be generous and forgive what happened over there.' He jerked his head towards the river. 'I'm afraid I lost my head, you ... you looked so lovely.' Sop to soften his withdrawal? He went on, and she sensed though she could not see his smile. 'Moonlight is responsible for an awful lot of folly—that's why madmen are called lunatics. Please forget my madness.'

As if she could ever forget the most devastating experience of her young life! But he had offered her a face-saver for her conduct as well as his.

'Yes, I know some people are affected by the moon.' She contrived to speak lightly. 'You and I must be among them.'

He gave an audible sigh of relief.

'And now we've returned to sanity. Come along in.'

He spoke in his usual tone of casual friendliness, so the episode at Memnon was to be obliterated. For him a moment of aberration, a yielding to a sexual urge, for her the awakening of an undying love.

As they came into the vestibule, she caught sight of a familiar figure standing by the reception desk. She had seen that trim safari-suited figure not so long ago. She turned to Miles.

'Isn't that Miss Orman?'

'Anna?' He threw her a wary look. 'It couldn't be.'

'It's someone very like her.'

But when she looked again the woman had gone.

'She's nowhere near Luxor,' he told her, suggesting he knew of Anna's movements. 'Like a drink?'

She refused, wanting only the solitude of her room.

'I'm tired. I'd like to go to bed.'

Was it her fancy or did he again look relieved?

'You must be, you've had a long day,' he agreed. Goodnight, my ...' he checked himself, '... Lorna. Sleep well.'

Though she was very tired, her troubled thoughts kept sleep at bay. In spite of his denial she was certain that it was Anna she had seen in the vestibule. Was it she Miles had gone to meet in the afternoon? If so, why couldn't he be open about it? He knew she was well aware of his friendship with 'his best girl-friend,' but perhaps he thought she might be annoyed if she knew she had turned up when he was escorting herself.

She recalled his fervent embrace and thrilled in retrospect. Miles was not indifferent to her, but he had indicated that the attraction was entirely physical. Certainly he had not wanted to go any further, when he had pushed her away. Was it because he was determined to show her that he could behave like a gentleman, as he put it, or because he owed loyalty to Anna?

Such scruples were old-fashioned in this day and age and she must have betrayed how much she wanted him. He had not availed himself of the opportunity she offered, not, she felt sure, from lack of inclination, but because some obstacle, real or imaginary, had intervened. It was ironic that she, who had never desired a man before, should have fallen for one who seemed determined to renounce her. But that was life, and tomorrow would bring another of those desolating partings with no certainty of further contact.

But first there was Karnak. She might during the morning manage to elucidate what there was between Miles and Anna and whether there was any hope for herself. And that would be in bright sunlight, with no moon to promote any further folly.

At last she fell asleep and dreamed of giant figures in the moonlight and Miles' kisses, only in her dream the colossi turned their battered faces towards her with a warning in their stony eyes.

In the morning there was a note on her tray with her morning tea. It read:

'So sorry, Lorna, I've further business to transact this morning—this was a business trip, I told you. I've arranged with a party going to Karnak to take you with them. Mr Knight will contact you. Don't miss it. M.'

Her first impulse was not to go, but when Mr Knight rang her on the house phone to tell her when they were starting, she realised that she must. What possible excuse could she give to Miles for staying put? A headache was too feeble—besides, she wanted to see Karnak, didn't she? A little inner voice whispered, 'Not without Miles,' but that was ridiculous. She had wanted to go to Karnak long before she had met Miles. Inevitably she connected Miles' desertion with Anna's appearance on the previous night. He must have seen her after she had gone to bed last night and this morning appointment was the result of their meeting. Possibly he had not known Anna was in the vicinity until she had made her presence known. It might also be that she had some interest in his new activities, as had occurred to her before. But whatever it was it was no business of hers. Dismally she reflected that she had no claim upon Miles nor any right to pry into his affairs, or his connection with Anna. She had merely come along for the ride. But she had expected Miles would find time to show her the sights, and he had again gone off leaving her to her own devices. There was no help for it: she would have to go to Karnak with Mr Knight's party.

When Lorna got there, she was temporarily lifted out of her preoccupations. Karnak to the north of

Luxor was tremendously impressive, though nothing remained of the gardens, houses and palaces which had once surrounded the temples. Approached by an avenue of ram-headed sphinxes, it was a complex of buildings, added to and altered during many periods. In the centre was the largest of all Egyptian temples, also dedicated to the Theban state god, Amon-re. There were ten pylons, those monumental piles which flank Egyptian entrances, a pillared hall of fourteen columns seventy-eight feet high, with raised roof slabs so that light and air could enter through this clerestory, and lateral aisles on either side. The pillars were enormous and all inscribed with hieroglyphics. The hypostyle hall was partly restored and three thousand years old.

But Lorna's attention was only perfunctory, her thoughts turning again towards Miles. She was sure that he had meant to show her Karnak himself, and only Anna's presence had deterred him. What hold had that plain but forceful woman got over him that she had only to beckon and he would go to her, whatever else he had intended? She had a nasty suspicion that the expedition was in the nature of an assignation and Miles' pretence that Anna was distant only a blind. Perhaps there were reasons why they had to meet in secret and he had brought Lorna along with him to provide a false trail. The expedition to view the colossi had been to fill in time and provide him with a temporary distraction, the seduction of moonlight and a sexual urge had caused him to go further than he had meant, but he was in reality waiting for Anna. Anna was no beauty, but she was poised and sophisticated, a more congenial companion for an experienced man like Miles than her ingenuous self. Child, he had called her when in her simplicity she had asked if he loved her ... a little. How could she have been such a naïve fool! Now he was probably regretting that he had brought her, since her juvenile passion for him might cause complications. He had expected her to be absorbed in sightseeing and not to notice what was going on. Yet she was sure that his motive in inviting her had been a genuine kindness on his part in conjunction with Bob Hailey. He knew she had no one to go about with and that she would have been alone in Cairo that weekend. He was kind and generous, but that was not what she wanted from him. However, she could not hope for more than the crumbs he spared her from Anna's feast, and his kisses in the moonlight had only been the natural reaction between a young man and a girl in romantic circumstances. He had been highly relieved when she had agreed to forget them.

I thought myself above such folly, she told herself ruefully. I really must grow up. The truth is I've been too secluded under Aunt Augusta's protection. I must regard Miles as part of my adult education. At least he did me no real harm, as he could have done had he been a heel.

A sage reflection which did nothing to comfort the heartache caused by his defection. She even caught herself wishing he had been more of a cad, but she knew temporary fulfilment would not have been enough. If she had Miles at all she wanted him for keeps, and without the shadow of Anna in the background.

The Karnak tour arrived back at the hotel in time for lunch and Miles was waiting for her. He was interested to know what she had thought of the place.

'A great pity I couldn't go with you,' he sounded genuinely regretful, 'but duty had to come first.'

Was duty another name for Anna?

He was exuding a sleek satisfaction which might have been the result of a deal successfully concluded or a pleasant interlude with 'his best girl-friend.' Lorna could not resist enquiring:

'Did you contact your colleague?'

He gave her a swift wary glance which confirmed her suspicions.

'Mission completed,' he said lightly, and changed the subject. 'I wish we had time to visit the Valley of the Kings. You'd like that. Perhaps another time.'

Would there be another time?

In the afternoon they returned to Cairo. The aircraft followed the course of the Nile, a blue streak far below with its belt of green on either side meandering through sandstone cliffs and patches of alluvial plain, with desert stretching to the horizons on either side.

Lorna chatted gaily throughout the short journey, determined to show Miles that she had not a care in the world, but he was unresponsive. Occasionally he turned his head and gave her a bleak look. She concluded that he was depressed by having to leave his beloved, and found her frivolous talk irritating. That was just too bad, but she had no intention of pandering to his gloomy mood, he would have to put up with her chatter.

When they came to part at the airport, she to returned to the Hilton, he to go she did not know where, she thanked him and Bob profusely.

'It was a wonderful experience,' she enthused.

'I'm glad you enjoyed it,' he said perfunctorily. A sudden gleam came into his so blue eyes. 'All of it.'

'All of it,' she declared brightly, guessing to what he referred but resolved to give no sign.

'Good.' His gaze travelled past her searching the crowd as if he were looking for somebody. Anna?

He put her in a taxi, saying vaguely: 'I'll be getting in touch with you some time. Until then, goodbye.'

'Goodbye,' she echoed, thinking it was the most hateful word in the language.

He did not wait to see her go but strode purposefully away, to be swallowed up by the crowd. Lorna felt sure he had already dismissed her from his mind.

Enigmatical, disturbing personality! But his elusiveness was part of his charm.

Lady Augusta returned from Alexandria in an irritable frame of mind.

'I'm an altruist,' she told Lorna, 'not a politician, but politics creep into everything nowadays. If ever there was an impediment to progress it's politics. I was baulked in every way.'

'I'm sorry, Aunt Augusta,' said Lorna, deducing the conference had not gone well.

'Much good your sorrow will do to anyone,' her aunt snapped. Then her voice softened. 'You look tired, child, your trip hasn't done you any good. Too hot and crowded, I expect, but I did warn you.'

Lorna let that pass. It was not the trip which was making her look wan.

'Getting very hot,' Lady Augusta went on, fanning herself vigorously with a newspaper she had picked up. 'We must go back to England soon, though the papers say the weather there is vile as usual. At least here it hardly ever rains.'

Lorna's heart sank. England. Separated from Miles by leagues of sea and land. But perhaps it would be best, far from this exotic land she might be able to get him out of her system, and it would seem she would need to do so, for days passed and she did not hear from him. He must have decided to drop her. He might have left Egypt for all she knew, as she herself would shortly be doing.

Hoping to encounter him, while despising herself for her weakness, she went several times to the Egyptian Museum. She walked among the huge granite statues of departed royalty rescued in many cases from the temples she had visited to save them from being broken up by the local people in days when they had not learned their tourist potential. She lingered by Anubis, recalling Miles upon that day when she had met him there, and the glad light of welcome in his eyes. He had cared, she thought feverishly, he must have cared ... a little, but she could not compete with Anna. The black jackal seemed to regard her with a satirical eye. There's only one certainty, the tomb, he seemed to be saying. The tomb where I presided over the last rites.

Lorna shivered and passed on to other items in the golden hoard. The splendid mummy mask of Tutankhamen mocked her with its sublime serenity. The frets and tribulations of earth were over for its wearer long ago.

But Lorna never saw Miles.

Then she did encounter one of his former associates. It was in the street one afternoon. There was the usual crowd on the pavement and she nearly collided with Bob Hailey. He recognised her at once, raising his hat, this time a linen one, from his bald head.

'Pretty as a picture,' he exclaimed, openly admiring her. 'And talking of pictures, you'll be glad to know that those shots of you on the horse came out real dandy.'

Lorna gave a little gasp. So the cinema public would be able to gape at her struggle with Miles.

'We worked it fine,' Bob went on. 'No one 'ud guess you weren't Rosie.'

That was one consolation, though she still felt dismayed. She asked if the Excelsior Company were still in Egypt.

'Packed up long ago,' he told her. 'I'm only here to fix some bits and pieces left outstanding.' The crowd jostled them. 'Look, we can't talk here—come and have a drink, a coffee or something.'

She went with him because it occurred to her that he might have news of Miles. Surely he would mention him sooner or later? Seated at a table at one of the pavement cafés, he meandered on about this and that until in desperation she asked:

'Do you ever hear from Mr Faversham?'

'Nary a word,' he dashed her hopes. 'The guy seems to have disappeared.'

The coffee was brought and he piled his cup up with sugar.

'Now there was a rum cuss,' he remarked thoughtfully. 'D'ye know, miss, I could've made a star out of that guy. He'd got looks, class, everything, and he was photogenic. But he wouldn't consider it. Shoved off when you did and never a word since.'

He drank his coffee and Lorna played with her teaspoon.

'Kept hoping he'd show up again,' Bob went on. 'He knew where he could find me, and when you're on your uppers fame and fortune ain't to be sneezed at, but he never did. There's only one way I can explain it, he was an alcoholic.'

'No!' Lorna exclaimed vehemently.

'Shocked you, eh? Why else was he so indifferent to success?' Lorna thought that not everyone wanted to be a film star, but did not say so, as Bob evidently thought it was the apex of ambition.

'Mind you, he never let me down, but when he weren't needed, he'd be off on a jag. One of our lads saw him in Cairo one night, looking a thorough mess—only knew him by his eyes.'

Lorna could not for one moment believe Bob was right. Miles, clean-limbed, clear-eyed, could never indulge in such a habit, but she was not going to wrangle with Bob. She had remembered that she owed this kindly little man thanks for her expedition up the Nile and started to thank him. He looked puzzled.

'First I've heard of it. Oh, I know we did think you ought to have some sort of recompense, and perhaps Miles took it upon himself to do the necessary. So you went with him?'

The small grey eyes under the linen sun hat looked at her doubtfully.

'Yes, and I enjoyed it immensely,' she told him. 'Karnak was wonderful.' Why had Miles brought Bob into it? To allay her doubts? To persuade her to accept? But why go to so much trouble when subsequent events had shown that her company did not mean much to him?

'You're a nice girl,' Bob told her. 'Take my advice and don't get yourself latched on to that guy. Oh, I know he's a fascinating chap, but he won't do you any good.'

Lorna coloured; Bob meant well, but he was clumsy.

'I can take care of myself,' she said stiffly.

Bob chuckled. 'Independent like all modern chicks. I've got two of my own and do they give me a headache! No offence meant, miss. I'm only thinking of what's best for you. I'd hate you to be let down.'

'None taken,' she said with a wan smile, warmed by his genuine concern. 'Mr Faversham always behaved himself with me.' (Well, more or less). 'And I ... I've lost touch with him.'

'Just as well,' Bob declared heartily. 'Bet he's off on another binge.' Dismissing Miles, he plunged into a long account of his wife and family. Lorna listened patiently, divining that he was lonely.

She finished the coffee he had ordered for her and they parted amicably. Against her will his words kept recurring to her. Such an addiction would account for Miles' changing occupations, his apparent aimlessness, and for Anna's solicitude. She might be trying to reclaim him, she looked the sort of woman who would be a do-gooder, and he resented her schoolmarm manner while appreciating her efforts on his behalf. Bob being a man would know aspects of Miles which he would conceal from a woman.

Then Lorna dismissed the whole idea as quite preposterous. It did not fit in with what she knew of Miles, his unimpaired vitality, his obvious physical fitness. But she could not evade the fact that he did not mean to contact her again. His casual promise to get in touch with her had no more meaning than the 'Be seeing you' which often marked the terminal of a romance. She would have to learn to live without him, but in the short space of time that she had known him, she had changed so much that she hardly recognised herself.

CHAPTER SEVEN

A BREAK was caused in Lorna's normal routine when the Merediths came to spend the Easter holidays in Cairo. Lady Augusta postponed her plans for leaving until after their visit. Vera Meredith was a distant cousin of hers, so presumably she was Lorna's connection also, but though eager to claim kinship with a title, Vera, an inveterate snob, ignored the secretary.

'She's a frivolous fool,' Lady Augusta described her, 'but at least she had the good sense to marry a man who could keep her in comfort.'

'I thought you considered it was degrading for a woman to be kept by her husband.' Lorna could not resist an occasional dig at her aunt's prejudices.

'For a normal woman, yes, but Vera's such a moron she'd never be able to earn her living, and it's better George should keep her than that she should be a liability on the state,' Augusta declared.

Vera was bringing her two children, Patricia ten and Kenneth twelve, and had booked accommodation at the Nile Hilton. George had been left at home pleading a press of business. Mrs Meredith was a fluffy blonde, pretty in a dollish way and dressed very smartly. She was shallow and pleasure-loving and determined to sample all the entertainment Cairo had to offer, which was considerable. She was also out to pick up any accommodating escorts who presented themselves. Lorna found herself frequently called upon to amuse the children and take them upon excursions. She did not mind, she liked children, though these two were older than the ages she preferred. Patricia was very like her mother and had already acquired some of her snobbish notions; Kenneth was more likeable and jeered at his sister's pretensions, which did not make for harmony, and Lorna often had to intervene in their squabbles.

Naturally they wanted to see the pyramids of Gizeh and the Sphinx, which were within easy reach of Cairo, an expedition which did not appeal to their mother nor to Lady Augusta, so Lorna volunteered.

'Bless you, you're an angel,' Lady Augusta declared. 'I've seen them, of course, and once was quite enough.' So had Lorna, but she did not mind going again.

'Get a taxi there,' her ladyship went on, 'and give them tea at Mena House. I don't care what you spend so long as I don't have to go myself.' So a taxi was summoned and the trio set forth.

Both children were insistent that they must have a camel ride, and Lorna promised this should be arranged. She knew the drill, and told their driver to drop them at the camel enclosure and proceed up to the Pyramids to await their arrival and then take them on to the Sphinx.

Camels, ponies and carriages were for hire and all three were soon mounted on the grumbling beasts, which rose to their padded feet with audible protests and plodded out of the enclosure and up the rise which led towards the bulk of the Pyramids, which could be seen towering over the scene, followed by their djellabah clad owners.

The ride ended in front of the second Pyramid, and it was then that trouble arose. Lorna knew the correct charge, and tendered it, but the camel driver, who had noted their arrival by taxi and their well dressed appearance, demanded more. Lorna disliked haggling, but neither did she like being cheated. An argument arose and several of the camel man's friends came to support their colleague. They began to look threatening, realising Lorna had no man with her, and she had decided that she had better give in, when a familiar voice enquired:

'Having trouble?'

She swung round to meet the quizzical gaze of vivid blue eyes, and her heart seemed to stop and then begin to race. To meet him here of all unlikely places when she had despaired of ever seeing him again overwhelmed her.

'Oh, Miles!' she breathed, and could say no more. Colour suffused her face and her grey eyes shone with a glad light, betraying her joy at meeting him. Lean, bronzed, clear-eyed, he was obviously physically fit and gave the lie to Bob Hailey's unpleasant suggestion. This man could not have been indulging in dissipation and Lorna knew her faith in him had been justified.

Since she seemed to be stricken dumb, Miles dismissed her tormentors with a few sharp words in Arabic, having taken in the situation. They melted away and the little group was left standing together.

Lorna could hardly believe that he was really

there in the flesh; she had sought and longed for him for so many weary days, though she supposed in actual fact the time had not been nearly as long as it seemed. Moreover, he was alone, there was no sign of Anna, which caused her considerable satisfaction.

Miles was staring at her with a comical mixture of wistfulness and dismay, and it flashed into her mind that he was not at all pleased to have encountered her. The thought was painful, and before she could stop herself she had said reproachfully:

'I . . . I've been expecting to hear from you.'

He shifted his gaze from her face to his feet and told her:

'I've been very, very busy down in the south. I'm only paying a flying visit to Cairo, and it was hardly worth while contacting you.'

But he was here, apparently doing nothing, and intuitively she knew that he would not have rung her even if he had had all the time in the world. He had meant to drop her, and the knowledge increased her hurt. It must be because of Anna; she had probably accused him of two-timing her when they were in Luxor.

Whatever his reasons, he was lingering now as if he were loth to leave her, and though pride dictated otherwise, Lorna sought for an excuse to detain him if only for a few minutes, before he was gone again. Pride was no solace to the hunger in her heart.

Patricia intervened.

'Is this person a friend of yours?' she asked Lorna haughtily, and Lorna could have cheerfully slapped her. The little madam, daring to speak like that about Miles!

Apparently quite unruffled, Miles told her:

'We're old acquaintances. We shared a quite amusing adventure in the desert.' There was a spark of mischief in his eyes and Lorna recalled vividly his suffocating grip when he had held her on his horse. So that had been amusing, had it? 'How lucky I was here to assist you again,' he concluded.

'I could have dealt with them,' Kenneth said truculently.

'Of course you could,' Miles agreed, 'if you'd known Arabic.' He hesitated. 'What are you going to do now?'

Lorna explained about the waiting taxi and the Sphinx.

'Send him away,' Miles commanded. 'I have a car here, I'll take you.'

'But ...' Lorna began, astonished by this offer.

'You're too fond of that word,' he cut in, 'and you'd better let me protect you. You'll be pestered left and right to buy things you don't want. Much better allow me to deal with them.'

Pedlars were hovering round them holding up gew-gaws and other articles, chanting monotonously,

'Only one dollar—two, or three,' according to what they hoped to get.

Patricia, for all her superior airs, looked a little nervous.

'Please come with us, Mr ... whoever you are.'

'Miles, and you are called?'

'Miss Meredith.' Then catching Lorna's eye: 'I mean Patricia.'

'Patricia? What a nice name.' He smiled at her and Patricia was won.

Lorna was puzzled, wondering what had caused him to change his mind. She was sure he had intervened with reluctance and had meant to leave immediately, but now he was proposing to escort them when there was no real need. He had an oddly triumphant expression as if he had come to some decision which pleased him. Rejoiced that he was going to stay with them, Lorna thanked him politely, hoping she had not betrayed too much pleasure.

The taxi paid off, the two children clamoured to be allowed to explore the dark entry into the bulk of the Pyramid which was open to the public. Lorna warned them that there was nothing to see and the passage was uncomfortably low, but they looked unconvinced. Knowing they could come to no harm, Miles told them to run along and he and Lorna would wait for them.

The children disappeared and he suggested that they should sit on the lowest ridge of the Pyramid while they waited. They climbed up to it and seated themselves side by side on the rough stone, looking at the motley scene before them. This, like so much in Egypt, was a contrast of old and new. To their right, the first Pyramid lifted its pointed bulk into the hard blue sky. On the sandy space immediately below them were motor coaches disgorging their loads of passengers. Mingling with them as they came up the road were strings of camels carrying their tourist riders, their attendants in flowing robes which could have come straight out of a Bible picture. But the visitors' modern dress and the soft drinks stall were importations from another era.

Miles was watching Lorna's face with a hungry look, and he murmured below his breath, 'Kismet.'

Low as it was uttered, she caught the word, and turned her head towards him.

'Kismet? That means fate, doesn't it? Do you mean it was fated that we should meet today?'

'The Islamic faith teaches that everything is fated, and it's useless to try to avoid one's destiny.'

'Have you been trying to avoid me?' The words slipped out before she could check them, and she blushed vividly. 'But of course, you said you hadn't been here,' she tried to cover her blunder.

He looked at her gravely. 'Yes, I've been in Upper Egypt.' He smiled suddenly. 'And the first person I run into upon my return is you.'

She wanted to ask if the encounter had been unwelcome as she had surmised, but decided she might not like his reply. He was here now beside her and she would not spoil the harmony of the moment by raising painful issues. Searching for a topic which might interest him, she told him:

'I met Bob Hailey the other afternoon.'

'Did you really? What did he have to say?'

'More than I wanted to hear. He talked quite a lot about you. He believes your erratic ways are due to ... to ...'

She stopped, appalled at her temerity, and yet she would dearly like to have his confirmation that Bob was wrong.

'Go on, let's have it.'

'He thinks you're an alcoholic.'

Miles threw back his head and laughed heartily.

'Good old Bob! He couldn't understand why I didn't want a film career—thought there must be something wrong with me.' He sobered. 'That's not one of my vices, Lorna.'

'I couldn't believe it was.'

'My loyal little friend!'

'Am I really your friend, Miles?'

He laid his hand over hers where it rested upon her knees, and she quivered at his touch.

'Throughout eternity.'

Too exaggerated to be sincere. She gave a sharp sigh. 'I'm afraid it'll be nothing like as long as that. We'll be going back to England any day now.'

His fingers clenched over hers so hard that she thought her bones would crack. Then he withdrew his hand.

'So this is *ave atque vale*,' he said quietly.

'What's that mean? I'm not a linguist like you are.'

'Hail and farewell.'

Her heart seemed to plummet to her sandals.

'Oh, Miles,' she was beginning, when the children came scampering back, blinking in the strong light.

'There wasn't anything to see,' Kenneth said disgustedly as he swarmed up beside her. 'Not even a bat!'

Lorna refrained from saying I told you so, and Patricia exclaimed: 'Now for the Sphinx!'

Miles installed them in his car, the children in the back, and drove them the short distance to the famous monument.

Lorna had seen it before and found it disappointing. It was dwarfed by the Pyramids and sadly battered. Excavations were going on on one side of it with attendant litter and a shed had been erected with a galvanised roof. People, animals and vehicles thronged the waste ground between it and the town, which was encroaching ever nearer. In past days with nothing surrounding it but sand and silence it must have been much more impressive.

'No atmosphere now, is there?' Miles observed, divining her thoughts. 'The influx of the populace spoils it.'

'Well, I suppose they've every right to come,' she pointed out. 'If only there weren't quite so many of them.'

Since she knew a camel ride was on the agenda she wore trousers and a thin top. A white cloth hat protected her head and sunglasses her eyes. She looked very slim and youthful in her boyish garb, and Miles said abruptly:

'You're much too thin. Does that aunt of yours work you too hard?'

'Not at all. I expect it's the heat.' She tilted her glasses at him provocatively. 'Do you like your women all curves?'

He gave her a wicked look. 'They're more comfortable to embrace than bones.'

'Since I'm not a candidate for your embraces, my lack of them won't matter,' she said loftily.

'History might repeat itself,' he warned her. 'I found you quite adequate at Luxor, but I don't want you to fade away.'

His reference to that unforgettable night caused her to become confused, but the children demanding their tea caused a diversion.

'They've been promised it at Mena House,' she

explained. 'Will you join us, Miles?'

She expected him to refuse, but to her surprise he accepted her invitation.

'Since you'll soon be leaving, I must see all I can of you.'

That was much, much better, and eradicated her first impression that he regretted their meeting.

'Don't you ever go to England?' she asked as they walked back to the car, the children running on ahead.

'Now and then, but I never stay anywhere for long.'

She stopped and faced him squarely. 'Do you know, Miles, you're a most mysterious person? We've been quite a lot together and you know all about me, but you've told me hardly anything about yourself.'

'There's not much to tell,' he returned lightly. 'I've parents living in England whom I visit from time to time—I'm an only one like you are. I've a wandering foot and England's too tame for me. I've had various jobs, as you know, and my present one gives me an excuse to stay in Egypt, a place that has always fascinated me. That about sums it up.'

A very bare outline, and there was so much more that she wanted to know—whether he ever intended to settle down, and where Anna came into the picture. But it was useless to try to force his confidence; sufficient that he was here, beside her, and she would not allow conjectures and forebodings to spoil the present felicity.

Mena House was a fantastic place, decorated with huge Moorish arches surrounded by coloured light bulbs. The waiters were preparing dinner for an influx of tourists and did not welcome their request for tea. But Miles insisted upon speaking to the manager and the outcome was that they were conducted down a long passage to a private lounge and their order taken for sandwiches, tea and cakes.

'How did you manage it?' Patricia asked, suitably impressed.

'I couldn't let Lady Augusta Clavering's relatives be neglected,' he told her.

Patricia preened herself, feeling important, but Lorna did not believe it was only her aunt's prestige that had won them preferential treatment.

The children had completely accepted him. Patricia, a coquette in embryo, had succumbed to his smile. Kenneth capitulated when he learned that Miles had played rugby for his school.

That achievement did not seem to fit in with his subsequent attempt to become a film actor, but about that Lorna kept quiet. She knew it would not recommend him to Lady Augusta.

'Of course that was a long time ago,' Miles remarked. 'Rugger is a young man's game.'

'And now you're nearly in your dotage,' Lorna said tartly.

'He hasn't any grey hairs,' Patricia objected.

Miles ran a hand over his smooth brown head.

'If you look very close you may find some.'

Patricia immediately jumped off her chair and proceeded to investigate.

'You asked for that,' Lorna told him.

'I did, didn't I?' He jerked his head back. 'What are you doing, child? Looking for nits?'

Child, and he had called Lorna child also upon

occasion. He must regard them both as a pair of infants.

'Of course I'm not!' Patricia declared, a little shocked. 'Your hair's ever so soft and fine and there are no grey hairs.'

'Then you'd better sit down.' Lorna spoke sharply, moved by a stab of unworthy jealousy. She wanted to feel his hair beneath her own fingers, and despised herself for the wish. Perhaps Miles was right, she was still very juvenile.

'How's the business going?' she went on, recalling Miles' latest occupation.

'Flourishing.'

'You don't seem to be working today.'

'This happens to be my afternoon off,' he said airily, contradicting his former assertion that he had no time to spare.

'Do you work here?' Kenneth eyed him curiously. In his experience English people only came to Egypt for holidays.

'Oh, definitely. I deal in antiques and curios.'

Kenneth looked disgusted. 'How dull!'

'You mean you serve in a shop?' Patricia asked disdainfully.

Miles laughed, stretching his long legs out before him.

'Can you see me behind a counter?'

'No, I can't,' the child replied. 'You look a lot better than that sort of person.'

Miles laughed again at this disparaging of shop assistants. He told her: 'I said I deal. That means I'm a sort of agent, I receive ... er ... goods and pass them on to people who require them.'

He spoke so frankly that Lorna was sure this was

an exact description of his activities.

'What sort of goods?' Kenneth demanded. His eyes gleamed hopefully. 'Guns?'

Lorna felt a moment's disquiet. There were so many kinds of goods, but Miles' next words reassured her.

'Gun running is illegal. My business is above board. I'm in Cairo to attend the sale of a defunct collector's effects which takes place tomorrow morning, and I hope to pick up some bargains.'

It sounded perfectly straightforward and Lorna sighed with relief. She did not know what she had been imagining, something illicit, she supposed, like Kenneth's guns or drugs, but she had no grounds for such suppositions except that Miles did not look like a business man and it seemed a tame sort of occupation for his restless spirit, but he said it entailed travelling, so that must be the attraction. She saw he was watching her with an amused smile as if he guessed her thoughts, and she had a suspicion that he enjoyed mystifying her.

The food consumed, they had no excuse to linger and reluctantly Lorna said they must be going.

'I'll drive you back, of course,' Miles insisted.

Lorna forbore to suggest they could easily call a taxi. She was greedy for every moment of Miles' company and perhaps when they came to part he would propose a further meeting.

He drew up in the forecourt of the hotel, and the children after murmuring their thanks ran inside, but Lorna hesitated. She thanked him effusively, prolonging their leavetaking. Was this to be only another indefinite parting, perhaps a final one? She held out her hand and he took it in both of his. She became aware of a subtle change in him, as if some barrier had been removed. There was a new purpose about him and his eyes were tender as he met the unspoken appeal in hers. Then she knew it was going to be all right; he would not leave her again in limbo, he was going to arrange another meeting.

'So you're back, Lorna? Where are the children?'

The shrill voice cut through their moment of communication like the slash of a knife. Neither had noticed the taxi draw up beside Miles' car, nor Vera Meredith descend from it, all frills and flutter. She had seen them at once and rushed up to them without waiting to pay her fare. She stood staring at Miles, her pale blue eyes in her vacant face avid with interest.

Miles dropped Lorna's hand and she turned to tell Vera the children had gone inside. Why had she had to intervene at such a moment? Now Miles would go off without speaking the words which she had longed to hear, and he might have second thoughts about contacting her. She saw he was staring at Vera with a guarded expression, which might be either admiration or repulsion. No, she decided firmly, he can't be attracted by a doll like her. But there was no doubt that Vera was taken with Miles.

'A friend of yours?' she asked Lorna, raising her pencilled brows, evidently astonished that Lorna could produce someone so presentable.

'Yes,' Lorna said shortly. 'Mr Faversham. Miles, this is Mrs Meredith, a relation of my aunt's, who is staying here.'

'The mother of those delightful children?' Miles enquired.

Vera laughed affectedly. 'They make me seem old, but I married very young.' She held out a well manicured hand. 'Delighted to meet you, Mr Faversham, but must we be so formal? My name's Vera ...?' She paused, but Miles said nothing. 'But why are we all standing here? Do come in, Mr Faversham, and have a drink or something.' She glanced at Lorna. 'I think you ought to go and see what the children are doing.'

Miles had taken Vera's hand and held it rather longer than was necessary, Lorna thought. Vera did look rather dashing in her white and red trouser suit, and she was definitely chic. Lorna had never seen Miles with any other woman except Anna, who compared unfavourably with Vera's femininity. He probably liked fluffy blondes, but to her relief he said:

'I'm sorry, but I'm afraid I can't stay.'

'Oh, but you must!' Vera pouted.

The taxi driver intervened, demanding his fare, and Vera turned to him impatiently, opening her handbag. Miles whispered to Lorna out of the side of his mouth: 'Don't go. I've something to ask you.'

After that no hint or even command of Vera's would have moved Lorna. She remained standing a little apart watching Vera's coquetry at work— the batting of artificially fringed eyelids, the swaying hips, the flutter of finger tips towards his sleeve.

'I can't let you run away when we've only just met,' she was saying. 'At least if you can't stay now, promise to call again. Perhaps this evening? Do you play bridge? Lorna doesn't, she's too stupid.'

Lady Augusta had wanted her niece to learn to play, and Lorna had tried, not very hard, to oblige.

She knew she would be continually called upon to make up a four if she proved proficient, and was highly relieved when she was pronounced a dud. But Vera's gibe rankled. She had little enough to recommend her to Miles without the implication of lack of brains.

'We haven't all got card sense,' Miles told her smoothly. 'Lorna's talents lie in other directions. I'm sorry, Mrs Meredith, I'm only staying a short while in Cairo and have no time for social engagements. However ...' a mischievous look came into his eyes, 'If you're interested in antiques, jewellery and so forth, I'm attending a sale tomorrow morning and perhaps you'd like to accompany me?'

Lorna could have laughed at Vera's startled expression if she had not been wounded by this invitation. He had never suggested that she might accompany him, and he knew she liked old things. But perhaps he thought Vera might be a potential customer.

'Are you interested in such things?' Vera asked incredulously.

'I deal in them. It's my trade.'

'You're joking!'

'I'm perfectly serious. You ask Lorna.'

'Oh, really!' Vera looked disgusted. 'I thought at least you were an Army man.'

'You're very perspicacious. I was a cadet ... once.'

Little by little Miles' history was being revealed. Lorna looked at him in surprise; she had never connected him with the Services.

'I suppose you were cashiered,' Vera said nastily. She was disappointed. She had thought from his car and his appearance, his casual clothes worn with distinction, and his air of authority, that she was on to a good thing, but if he was a mere tradesman, Lorna could keep him.

'You can't expect me to admit to that,' Miles told her. His blue eyes were brimming with mischief and Lorna realised he had been deliberately teasing Vera. He knew she would never come anywhere near a sale.

'Oh! Well then, I'll say good afternoon.' Vera flounced away. She looked back once, as if half inclined to return to the attack, then with a shrug went into the hotel.

Miles watched her retreat with laughter in his eyes.

'Very transparent person, Mrs Meredith,' he observed. 'But what an exhibition! Lorna, you could learn a lot from your friend.'

'She's no friend of mine,' Lorna told him tartly. 'And would you really like me to behave like that?'

'I would not. I prefer you as you are.'

'Well, that's something,' she said, a little mollified. 'But were you really cashiered, Miles?'

'I came out before they got round to doing that.'

'You ... you can't mean you deserted?'

He raised his head proudly. 'I don't desert, Lorna, I resign.'

'Oh, you're always teasing,' she cried. 'But really I'll have to go in. It's been a wonderful afternoon, Miles, and ...'

'You said all that before Flossie interrupted. Lorna,' he became serious and his voice deepened, 'have dinner with me tonight.'

'Oh, Miles, I wish I could,' she was distressed, 'but I can't. You know we've got visitors and I'm looking after the children ...'

'Have you added nursemaid to your other ploys?' he interrupted almost savagely. 'This is important.' His eyes glittered and he seemed to be labouring under some stress. 'I suppose they go to bed? When are you free, ten, eleven, midnight?'

'After dinner, tennish.'

'I'll be waiting here. You'll come?'

'I ... it'll be so late. Must it be tonight?'

'Yes, I can't wait any longer.' He smiled crookedly. 'Our meeting by the Pyramids decided me. One can't escape one's fate.'

Cryptic words, but Lorna dared not linger longer to question him. Vera would send someone to look for her, or tell Lady Augusta she was carrying on with a man. She had still to account to them for his appearance. But she could no more refuse his invitation than a needle can escape from a magnet.

'Yes, I'll come,' she promised. 'About ten o'clock.'

She went indoors on a surge of exhilaration. Miles was back, he had made a date with her after refusing Vera's overtures. Prudence, caution, self-preservation were thrown to the winds. He held her completely in thrall.

She sobered when she wondered what to tell her aunt, for of course the children would have chattered, and she was right. Lady Augusta called her into the sitting room soon after she had come in and regarded her with a dubious expression.

'The children tell me you found another knight errant by the Pyramids, and he brought you back.'

'Actually it was the same one.' Lorna found the explanation easy after all. 'He greeted me as an old friend and was very helpful.'

Lady Augusta had not met Miles so she would not know that he was young and attractive.

She gave Lorna a shrewd look.

'Don't get involved until you know his antecedents and prospects,' she warned. 'And if he's in the movie trade, I don't suppose they'll stand investigation. But you're too level-headed, I'm sure, to encourage someone undesirable.'

Prospects, antecedents? Lorna simply did not consider them.

There remained Vera to cope with, but it transpired that one of her most forthcoming escorts had called for her and she had gone out without informing Lady Augusta.

'I suppose George knows how she goes on when he's away,' Augusta remarked acidly to Lorna. 'But I expect he's as bad when he's on his own. Thank God I never married!' She went on to say that she would be playing bridge in the card room after dinner and Lorna would be on her own.

Nothing could have suited Lorna better.

She changed into a black dress and draped a black silk shawl over her head in which garb she would be inconspicuous. Then with her heart beating fast with eager anticipation, she crept out into the blaze of light which was Cairo by night.

CHAPTER EIGHT

MILES was parked in the same place where he had been in the afternoon. He did not get out when Lorna approached, but opened the passenger's door from the inside.

'Hop in and let's get out of here.'

Lorna gained the impression that he did not want to be seen. Possibly he feared another interception from Vera. Following that train of thought, she said:

'She's out.'

'Who's out? Oh, the painted doll.' He guided the car into the maelstrom of traffic. 'On the manhunt?'

'I think she's captured her quarry for tonight.' Then it occurred to her that she was being a little uncharitable, and she added: 'She has to amuse herself somehow, and if she likes men and men like her, who can blame her?'

'You don't, evidently, and myself, I'm all for living and let live, but I've not much use for those empty-headed types.'

Lorna recalled Anna, who whatever she was could not be termed empty-headed, but she instantly dismissed her from her mind. This was her night and she would not permit thoughts of Anna to intrude upon it. She was presumably far away and any claim she might have upon Miles was temporarily in abeyance. Nor would Lorna consider the future. Tomorrow Miles would go away again after the sale, but now he was beside her and he had said once he lived in the present, and so would she. She could not analyse this passion which had overwhelmed her, and overwhelm was the operative word. It was a force outside herself, too strong to be resisted. For the first time she could sympathise with all the heroines of romance who had had similar experiences, instead of being contemptuous of them. How did it go? 'Whoever loved that loved not at first sight?' Well, perhaps not quite at first sight, though she had felt his magnetic attraction from the first moment of meeting, and resented it. It was not until Luxor that she had learnt to know her own heart.

But Miles' feelings were still enigmatical. He must *like* her or she would not be with him now at his request; she knew she could arouse in him what he termed 'a sexual urge', but he had never said he loved her, or even that he was in love with her, which was not quite the same thing, in fact he seemed to be trying to resist whatever it was that had risen between them. She stole a look at him while the traffic was engaging all his attention, for after those few remarks about Vera he had to concentrate. The light from the street illuminated his strong profile, straight nose, wide brow and well shaped mouth above the firm chin. Lorna knew it all by heart, but she could never look long enough.

He drove through the town as fast as the traffic would allow. Brightly lit cafés and theatres swept by; handsome residences and humble homes, fine limousines and on the sandy verges, donkeys and donkey carts. Miles took the main road to Alexandria, not the desert route but the one which crossed the delta. Houses gave way to cotton and maize fields, trees, palms, olives and eucalyptus, mud-walled villages, their flat roofs stacked with sheaves of corn put there to dry and piles of rubbish giving them a derelict appearance. Here and there a faint light gleamed, but for the most part they were dark. The fellahin retired early to rest before another day of toil. In one place the railway ran parallel with the road, and the glowing serpent of a train sped past them. It was a starlight night without wind. The moon which had lighted them at Memnon had waxed and waned, the crescent that remained would not rise until the small hours.

At length Lorna ventured to break the silence between them which was becoming oppressive.

'Miles, where are you taking me?'

'Nowhere in particular.' He slowed the car. 'We'll turn off here.'

He took a narrow byway beside an irrigation canal in which the tall masts of moored feluccas with folded sails were stark against the sky. They passed a farm where a water buffalo used to pump water slept beside the scene of its daily toil. It raised a heavy head and grunted as they went past. Then amid silence and solitude. Miles stopped the car.

'A cigarette?'

'You know I don't smoke, but have one yourself if you wish.'

His lighter flared, and she saw the planes of his face were set and a little strained.

For a while he smoked in silence, then he said shortly:

'After Karnak I was resolved not to see you again.'

'Oh, Miles!' she cried in distress. 'Why? What had I done?'

'You hadn't done anything except be your alluring self. It was for your sake I decided we were better apart. But when I met you this afternoon by the Pyramids, I knew I couldn't ...' he struck the steering wheel to emphasise his words, 'put you out of my life.'

'But ... but did you have to?' Their faces were only pale blurs in the faint light which made it easier for her to speak. 'If only you knew how I've missed you! Your friendship means a lot to me, Miles.'

'Friendship?' He laughed harshly. 'Don't try and kid yourself with that myth. It isn't friendship you want, nor I either. Oh, you've been very circumspect, very modest, but you can't control your eyes, they speak for you, my darling, and their message this afternoon was plain to read.' He pushed his cigarette stub into the ash tray with a violent movement, and turning in his seat, took her face between his hands. 'I want you, Lorna, so much.'

His mouth came down on hers, gently at first but with increasing passion. His hands slipped behind her shoulders, drawing her near and his lips travelled her throat, her cheeks, her eyelids, and again fastened upon her mouth.

'Ah, Lorna,' he sighed against her ear. 'I'm mad for you.' And Lorna felt like a drought-stricken field drawing in the first rainfall for months. She laughed in rapturous delight.

'Sweet madness,' she said, and put up her hand to stroke his head, the smooth brown hair upon which Patricia's touch had roused her jealousy.

'Yes.' Gently he eased her back into her seat, and felt for another cigarette. Lighting it, he said: 'You know what this must lead to, Lorna?'

'Whatever you say. I'm utterly yours, to do with what you will.' She spoke recklessly, completely carried away, not caring how he would interpret her words, intent upon only one thing, to bind him to her so that he would not leave her again.

'Don't tempt me to be a blackguard,' he said harshly. 'I don't want just an affair, not with you, you're the wrong sort. You'd break your heart, and perhaps mine too.' He stubbed out the half-smoked cigarette. 'There's only one solution, you'll have to marry me.'

'M ... marry?' In her wildest dreams she had not gone as far as that. She remembered that he had told her he was not free, because he had other obligations. What had happened to them?

'You said once you had other commitments,' she reminded him.

'They can be disposed of ... in time. But they're no insurmountable obstacle. I propose to take you home to my parents. They'll welcome you gladly.' An acid note crept into his voice. 'They'd welcome anything that would keep me in England. They want me to get a steady job ...' he reached for yet another cigarette, '... produce children.'

'Don't you want children?' Lorna asked a little anxiously, for she did.

'Only if they're yours.'

Evidently there had been friction between him and his parents regarding his mode of life. She said doubtfully:

'You mean they didn't like you working in films?

But you've given that up, haven't you?'

'Definitely. I never took it at all seriously.'

'But shouldn't you? It's ... er ... more productive than trading ... I mean, if you have to support a family?'

'Always practical, aren't you, Lorna? Such a charming mixture, of romanticism and common sense. I suppose Bob talked to you about me, and you're imagining yourself married to a glamorous film star? I couldn't face that, even for you.'

'Miles!' She put her hands upon his shoulders and shook him, not very effectively, she had not the strength.

'I don't care what you do, it's you I love, but if we leave Egypt it'll be the end of your ... er ... business, and what else can you do?'

'You'd be surprised,' he laughed.

'Do be serious. I ... I only want you to be happy, Miles.'

'You'll make me that. Oh, Lorna!' He put his arm round her and pressed her against his side. 'There've been other women, you know, but none have ever touched my heart before. They were just transitory, casual affairs. There's something about you, apart from your looks, that appeals ...' He stopped, groping for words.

'Compatible chemistry,' she suggested.

'None of your smart modern jargon! It must be love.'

'Love? But can it really be that ... so soon?' she asked wonderingly. The practical side of her nature had taken over, and she knew infatuation was not love, she feared that was all Miles felt for her. She went on:

'That's a word I've always been afraid of. You see, my parents were very much in love, but they ended in divorce.'

'But they had many years together, didn't they?'

'Not long. The rot started soon after I was born. They lived under the same roof for my sake, but they were ... apart.'

'And so you're afraid that'll happen to us?'

'I think we shouldn't be in too great a hurry, we should make sure ...'

'Aren't you sure? I am. Oh, stop being a wet blanket, Lorna, all life's a gamble and I'm ready to stake everything on you. We want each other, isn't that enough? I'm prepared to give up everything for you.'

'Give up?' She pondered that. 'Give up what? Do you mean Anna?'

To her dismay he withdrew his arm, exclaiming:

'Oh, my God, I'd forgotten Anna! What am I going to say to her?'

Lorna felt cold. 'Is she so important to you?'

'She is and she isn't,' he said cryptically. 'She has on occasion been of great assistance to me. She's a strange woman—half Egyptian, of course. You saw that?'

'I'd only really seen her that time in your tent—no, I didn't realise she was half Egyptian.'

'And Egyptians are a mixed race. All sorts of strange genes went to make up Anna. I'd trust her with my life, but lately she's been a bit unpredictable.'

Lorna thought she had a notion as to why that was so. Anna for all her masculine traits was a woman. She regarded Miles as her property, and she would resent the intrusion of another woman into his life, and jealous women could be spiteful.

'Does she know how you feel about me?' she hazarded.

'Not this ... er ... latest development. And I do know she wouldn't want me to marry, because it would be the end of our work together.'

'I don't understand. If it really is flourishing, why need we go back to England? I could live out here.'

'You could not. Egypt isn't the right place for Nordic lilies. You'd wither in the hot seasons, and I couldn't bear to send you away once we're married.'

Lorna thrilled to hear him say it, but she had a feeling that he was making excuses, and that was not his real reason for wanting to leave the country.

'Miles,' she began earnestly, 'please tell me the truth. Is there more between you and Anna than a business partnership? I mean, if you're committed to her in any way it isn't right to walk out on her.'

He looked at her wonderingly, but he could see little of her face. Lorna's hands were clenched in her lap as she waited for his reply. It was in a way a test. If he could be moved by a sudden passion for her to the extent that he was ready to ditch poor Anna, who had a prior claim, it did not speak well for his constancy. Though her heart was urging her to take what he offered whatever the cost, some shred of sanity was warning her not to tie herself to a fickle man, for the outcome could only be future heartbreak. He had admitted that his decision to ask her to marry him dated from their meeting that afternoon; prior to that he had intended to drop her.

'These violent delights have violent ends,

And in their triumph die.'

The quotation recurred to her. She wanted a love that would last, not a sudden flare-up and ashes.

'So you consider that if I were engaged to Anna, which I'm not, we should sacrifice our happiness to a mistake?' he demanded. 'I don't think you can love me very much, Lorna.'

'Oh, I do, I do!' she cried desperately. 'But don't you see, you did introduce her to me as your best girl-friend.'

To her indignation, for she was in deadly earnest, he laughed.

'And that's been needling you ever since? Poor little Lorna, did you fear you were trespassing?'

'*Am* I?'

'No! There's nothing of that sort between Anna and me. She's been a loyal friend and colleague, that's all, so you can put your tender conscience to rest.'

'You swear it?'

'Cross my heart. Oh Lorna, Lorna, you've only to look at her. Poor Anna, she's not the sort of woman any man would want to take to bed.'

Privately Lorna had always thought Anna was an incongruous mate for Miles, and apparently he thought so too.

Somewhat relieved by his protestations, she asked provocatively:

'You prefer something more clinging?'

'Definitely, and if we weren't in the front of this car, which is not the best place for demonstrations, I would make you cling good and proper.' A passionate note sounded in his voice, then he seemed to restrain himself. 'Time enough for that when we're married, and we must be married soon. When I've settled up here, we'll fly back to England and get a licence. We can live with my parents until we can get a house of our own—they've got a big place and they only live in a part of it. Marlow. Do you know Marlow?'

She did. A pretty place by the Thames in the commuter country, but it did not seem the right setting for Miles, being too tame, too artificial. She supposed all her conceptions of him were coloured by their first meeting, the desert man on a horse.

'But what will you do there?' she asked, bewildered by his precipitancy.

'Make love to you, of course. No, seriously, Lorna, I'll have no difficulty in getting a job, and I've plenty of resources. Don't worry that I won't be able to keep you in the manner to which you're accustomed.'

She was not bothered about that at all. She did not desire riches, what is termed as a good match. If Miles were hard up, she would be quite willing to work herself to help with expenses, but she was troubled by his urgency. Surely it would be wiser for him to establish himself before they were actually married? She would have liked a little time to prepare herself for such a big change in her life, and to introduce him to her aunt. She could not rid herself of the feeling that his proposal was the result of their unexpected meeting, and he was planning wildly to meet an eventuality he had not foreseen.

'Is there any reason for such haste?' she asked doubtfully.

'Lorna, do you or do you not want to marry me?'

'Oh, I do, I do, but ...'

'Your favourite word,' he jeered. 'There are no buts about it. You leave all the arrangements to me, and keep mum yourself. I'll not have the noble Lady Augusta Clavering wafting you off to some unknown destination after preaching marry in haste and repent at leisure. I know quite a lot about your aunt—sour old virgin.'

'Miles, that's not kind. She's been very generous to me.'

'She's had good value out of you.' His voice deepened. 'I'll be good to you, Lorna, and once you're mine your slightest wish shall be my law. But I want to make sure of you first.'

Lorna had her reservations about that. She could not imagine Miles being a doting husband. He would always rule his life and hers, and she would prefer it that way. Contrary to Lady Augusta's teaching, she believed a man should be master in his own house.

'You are sure of me,' she told him earnestly. 'There'll never be anyone else for me but you— I knew that at Luxor. Since you came riding into my life ... I ... haven't been the same since.'

'The damage to me was done when I saw you lying on that miserable camp bed in my tent. Such a lovely delicate-looking being, crying out for love and protection.'

'Oh, I wasn't!' Lorna was always a little annoyed when he assumed what she termed his frail lily act. She was a normal healthy girl and strong enough to be a good wife and mother.

'I've always been able to stand on my own feet,' she told him firmly.

'You won't have to any more, Lorna, we'll be together always.'

He bent forward and kissed her lips, not fiercely demanding but gently and tenderly. Lorna put her arms round his neck and buried her face in his pull-over. She could feel his heartbeat against her cheek, a little rapid but strong and steady. He put his arms about her and held her close, and she felt she had found safe haven.

About them was the stillness of the Egyptian night, so windless that the grunt of the buffalo was audible in the quiet as he moved restlessly on his straw. Above them were the great shining stars.

Presently Lorna lifted her head.

'When do you propose to leave for England?'

'Within a few weeks. First I must go south to wind up the business.'

'How long will that take?' she asked anxiously, hating the thought of parting with him again.

'A week, possibly two. So you'll have a little while to get used to the idea of entrusting your future to me.'

'Couldn't I come with you?'

'My dear Miss Travers, I seem to remember some maidenly scruples about spending a night with me in a hotel in Luxor, although we had separate rooms, and it'll be much more difficult now.'

'It won't matter now we're engaged.'

'You think not?' he asked in a curious voice. 'No darling, we won't jump the gun.'

She had not meant quite that, but evidently he could no longer trust himself.

'Seriously though, Upper Egypt would be getting much too hot for you now,' he added.

'I don't mind heat—and I'd like to know how you spend your time.'

'Oh, would you?' Then he said a strange thing. 'All my future is yours, darling, but I must finish off my past alone.'

She drew away from him.

'Do you know, Miles, there's a cloak and dagger touch about this business of yours. You wrap it up in mystery.'

She felt him tense beside her, then he said casually:

'You're being romantic again. Continual bartering and haggling can become very monotonous.'

'You're the most unlikely person to be a merchant.'

He laughed. 'What about the merchant adventurers? Don't you know trade penetrates further than exploration? Trade won India for Britain, though she has since lost it. Isn't that romantic?'

'Oh very, but the days of colonialism are past, and you'll be seeing Anna Orman.'

'How you do go on about poor old Anna! Don't you trust me?'

'Yes, but ...'

'Oh, to hell with your buts!' he broke out impatiently. 'Look, Lorna, I'm only going to settle up a few outstanding matters and find another agent to help Anna. *Do* you trust me?'

'Of course. What's love without trust?'

'Quite a lot,' he said wryly. 'But it can be hell.'

'So I should suppose.'

He had asked for her trust, but had he been

straight with her? She had an intuition that he was concealing something from her that had to do with Anna. He had sworn that there was nothing between them—but men were not always honest about their affairs with other women. There might have been a time when he had not found Anna so unattractive, they were old friends apparently, and though he had chosen to forget, Anna would not, and he was going to see her again and tell her he was about to marry someone else. How would she take it? Not lying down, Lorna thought, and she would do all in her power to make him change his mind. In her power? Had she any hold over Miles? At one time it had seemed she had, but not now, surely not now.

Unaware of her doubts and fears which Lorna dared not express, for she was sure he was confident he had allayed them, Miles said cheerfully:

'Having settled everything, I'm afraid I must take you back. It's getting very late.'

'And I shan't see you again before you leave? Wouldn't you have time to call upon my aunt?'

'Dear Lady Augusta!' he laughed. 'She'll have to wait until I come back. I leave directly after the sale.'

'Couldn't I come to that? You asked Vera.'

'Only to put her off. I'm afraid it'll be strictly men only.'

'You *will* be back in a week?'

'I hope so. Two at most.'

'You'll write?'

'My dear girl, I'd be back before the letter arrived. Cheer up sweetheart, what's a week?'

'Or two?'

'We'll hope it won't be that. Kiss me again and then we must go.'

Closely held in his arms with his lips on hers, Lorna felt her confidence return. Or more correctly her senses swamped her reason. With such an intensity of passion between them, surely they had been made for each other and nothing could come between them.

They drove back into the whirl of Cairo night life, and when they reached the hotel, she asked wistfully:

'You could come in and see Aunt Augusta now, and tell her we're engaged.'

She felt that if only he would do that, he would give reality to a happening which by morning might seem to be a dream. She wanted her aunt to meet Miles before she broke the news to her, for she knew that the account she would have to give of him would not seem satisfactory to that critical person.

He looked at the luminous dial of his watch and exclaimed:

'My darling, at this hour! She'll have gone to bed, or if she hasn't she won't be very receptive to our news. I mean, if we're going to meet opposition there it can wait until my return. I wouldn't want you to have to live with it for a week without my support.'

He had a point there. Lorna had no idea how Lady Augusta would react, and if she was difficult it would make the waiting time even more unbearable.

'Then I won't say anything until you're here to face her with me,' she decided.

'That might be wise,'

He kissed her again before she got out of the car, long and lingeringly, and then he said:

'If something unforeseen should occur, you'll wait? I'll come back to you in the end, though, in the words of the poet, all hell should bar the way.'

This seemed an echo of her own forebodings and she cried anxiously:

'Oh, Miles, you don't mean you might be delayed?'

'Most unlikely.'

'Accidents do happen,' she said fearfully.

'Then you would be advised.'

'Should I? Can't you give me an address where you can be found?'

'I'm afraid not. I'm always on the move, I'll be going from village to village, our contacts ... clients, have to be paid for their handicrafts and advised of my departure. I'll not be more than a night here and there.'

'But in Cairo ...?'

'Lorna, I have no permanent address except in Marlow, I never have had one out here.'

'But Miles, Aunt Augusta is leaving soon, she might even decide to return with the Merediths before your second week is up. What'll I do then?'

'Nothing, I'll do the necessary. Give me your London address, and I'll follow you.'

She told him the number of the Mayfair flat which was Lady Augusta's English home. He repeated it as if to fix it in his memory.

'I could write it down if you've got a pencil and paper.'

'No need, it's engraved upon my heart,'

She disliked such gallant utterances, they always seemed to her to be insincere, but Miles said it as if he meant it. He was waiting for her to leave him, but she could not tear herself away. She ought to have been deliriously happy, and if Miles had been staying in Cairo she would have been, but the prospect of his imminent departure filled her with unreasoning foreboding.

'If only you didn't have to go away!' she burst out.

'Aren't you making rather heavy weather out of nothing?' he asked patiently. 'I'll be back almost immediately. Don't think I don't hate leaving you, every minute away from you will seem an hour, but it can't be helped. Soon there'll be no more partings, we'll be together always. Now you really must run along, tomorrow will be a day to cross off the calendar, one less. Goodnight, beloved.'

She clung to him in one last embrace, and then very gently he disengaged himself, and pushed her out of the car, not offering to escort her to the door. Lorna ran blindly across the forecourt to the entrance, and when reaching it, she looked back, his car was gone. The empty space where he had parked seemed to mock her. Had it ever been there? She rubbed her eyes to rid herself of the curious illusion that the events of the evening had never taken place. She had nothing concrete to hold on to as evidence of its reality. She ought to have asked him for some token in place of the ring which presumably he would give her upon his return; surely among his merchandise he would have had some small article which she could have treasured. The only thing she had that he had given her was Anubis stamped upon the piece of papyrus, and with a shudder she remembered that Anubis was associated with the dead.

CHAPTER NINE

THE days passed. Lorna did as Miles had suggested, cross each one of them off the calendar while despising herself for her childishness. He had left on a Wednesday and she ringed the next one in red. Then as an afterthought she ringed the one after. He had said it might be two weeks. The Merediths went back home, and Lady Augusta had played with the idea of returning with them, to Lorna's disquiet. But she changed her mind and their departure was scheduled for the end of April over a fortnight ahead. Cairo was becoming very hot.

Several times Lorna looked speculatively at her aunt and debated whether she would confide in her, but decided to wait for Miles. When he came she would have to point out to him that she could not walk out on her job at a moment's notice. She would have to give Lady Augusta time to replace her, but she did not think he would be unreasonable. Perhaps they could all go back to London together, herself an engaged girl, and make the normal arrangements for her wedding. She would be content with a very quiet one; Miles, like many men, probably shrank from a big do, but she would like to be married in church, it seemed more binding.

On Sunday night she crossed off the day, noticing with joy that there only remained two more before she could expect Miles, if he came within the week. At least she would have the glad expectation of seeing him any day after that. On Monday morning she had a visitor.

Reception rang the suite to tell her that there was a lady wanting to see Miss Travers.

'Did she give her name?'

'No, but she says that you're acquainted with her and she must see you alone.'

'I am alone,' Lorna verified, for her aunt was out; she was rarely in in the morning after she had attended to her mail.

It must be some hanger-on of Lady Augusta's, she supposed, who hoped to ingratiate herself with the secretary, but when in response to the knock upon the door she said 'Come in,' it was Anna Orman who appeared.

She was wearing a dark red trouser suit and was bareheaded. To Lorna, now she knew, her Eastern blood was very apparent in her black hair, narrow eyes and the supple way she moved. Her hard brown eyes glanced scornfully round the room.

'What a Ritzy palace,' she remarked. 'Quite a little hothouse flower, aren't you, Miss Travers?'

'I'm a working girl,' Lorna contradicted her. 'Actually a poor relation of Lady Augusta's.' It suddenly occurred to her that Anna, and possibly Miles also, thought she had expectations, and it was a distasteful idea. 'Sit down, Miss Orman,' she went on, 'and tell me what I can do for you.'

Anna sat down on the hardest chair she could find. Evidently she despised luxury.

'I expect you're surprised to see me,' she said shortly.

'Well, I am,' Lorna admitted. Sudden hope illuminated her pale face. 'Have you brought a message from Miles?'

'He's not in a position to send you messages.'

Fear shot through her. 'He's ill? Hurt?'

'Not as far as I know, but he'll not be returning to Cairo, Miss Travers.'

The pupils of Anna's eyes had expanded until her eyes were all black and they glittered, while her thin mouth curved venomously. Lorna knew that she disapproved of her friendship with Miles and she suspected Anna meant to break it if she could, and was prepared to do battle for him. She said calmly:

'I would find that more convincing if he told me so himself.'

'No doubt,' the other woman snapped. 'Nevertheless it's true.' Her glance swept over Lorna's slight figure in her cool white dress. 'You're very pretty, Miss Travers, just the fragile, delicate sort of beauty that would appeal to a masculine man like Miles. But I won't allow him to throw himself away upon you.'

'I fail to see what it has to do with you,' Lorna exclaimed, feeling thoroughly nettled. 'Surely that's something Miles has to decide for himself. You're jealous, aren't you? You want him yourself and you can't bear to give him up to me.'

She spoke with more confidence than she felt. She had always suspected there was some bond between Miles and this woman, but she was not going to allow herself to be intimidated. If she were sufficiently blunt, Anna might be provoked into explaining their association.

'No, I can't,' Anna confirmed. 'Oh, I know I'm

not the sort of woman men fall in love with, but I've worked with Miles for some time. He respects me, he has a considerable liking for me—not what I want, naturally, but it's something. I'm not going to be supplanted by a fluffy little social parasite who like as not will let him down in the end.'

Lorna flushed angrily. 'You've no right to insult me, Miss Orman. I'm not a parasite, I told you I work for my living, though my employer is my aunt and my surroundings may seem opulent. I was left on my own at sixteen and Lady Augusta had me trained ...'

'I'm not interested in your life story,' Anna cut in insolently, 'but in extricating Miles from your clutches.'

'What do you think I am?' Lorna demanded heatedly. 'I wouldn't want to clutch Miles against his will.' Her voice softened and her big grey eyes grew tender. 'We love each other, Miss Orman, and we're going to be married.'

A dull red flush rose to Anna's cheeks and she drew back her head like a snake about to strike. Her eyes were malevolent.

'Rather sudden, isn't it?' she asked nastily. 'He'd no thought of marriage when I saw him in Luxor not long since, though it was obvious he was making a fool of himself over you. He should never have taken you there.'

So it had been Anna Lorna had seen in the hotel vestibule, though Miles had declared she was far away, and the first faint element of doubt began to stir. Why had Miles pretended she was not there?

'I hoped he would have got over his infatuation by now,' Anna went on. 'You've seen him since?'

'Before he left for the south, but weren't you to have met him there? To ... to wind up your business?'

Anna threw back her head and laughed harshly.

'So that's what he told you? To wind up our business? Yes, I am to meet him down there to-morrow, but first I wanted to have a word with you, to warn you off.'

'Oh, did you!' Lorna was really angry now. She had been inclined to feel some sympathy for Anna. Her words had confirmed what he had said about her, that there had been no love passages between them, and if she loved him his indifference must have made her suffer. But her present attitude was insufferable.

'You haven't known him long,' Anna was saying. 'If you had, you'd know he's unreliable. You mustn't believe any promises given in a sudden burst of passion, which I suppose is what provoked them. You don't really know what kind of man he is at all—how could you in so short a while? You shouldn't believe anything he says.'

Her black eyes were cunning and Lorna was sure she was deliberately maligning Miles.

She said firmly: 'You can't destroy my faith in him.'

'Then you're a fool,' Anna snapped. 'You aren't the first with him and you won't be the last. If you're expecting him to return to you you'll be disappointed. He won't come back.'

'I don't believe you.' But in spite of her bold front, Lorna's doubts were growing. She walked to the window and looked out unseeingly at the river. There had been no need for Miles to offer her marriage. In the wild ecstasy of their reunion she had been his for the taking, that he had declared they must marry had shown his innate decency, but as he had said, they had both been mad that night, drunk with the rapture of being together after separation. Anna was right up to a point, she should not have taken seriously any protestations made evoked by the magic of the Egyptian night. Miles had confessed that he had intended to renounce her until their chance meeting had shattered his resolutions. Now he was away from her again, he might be regretting his offer.

Anna watched the slim, drooping figure as a cat watches a mouse it is playing with before it delivers the *coup de grâce*.

'You're very young,' she said almost kindly. 'You'll be returning to England shortly, won't you? Oh yes, I know that, Lady Augusta's movements are public knowledge. There you can forget all this, find a man of your own class who won't let you down. These violent passions never last, they flare up and die.'

Lorna winced inwardly. She knew that could be true, yet whatever Miles felt for her, her own emotions went much deeper. Coming dramatically into her life, he had imprinted his image indelibly upon her heart and imagination. She was unlikely ever to meet anyone to compare with him, and she had always hated second best.

She swung round to face the other woman.

'I will only believe Miles wasn't in earnest if he tells me so himself.'

Again Anna laughed. 'My dear, you're exposing your lack of sophistication. That's something no man will ever tell a woman. He'll only prevaricate, if you see him again, which you won't. He knows it's best you should separate, and he has work to do here in Egypt in which you'd only be an impediment.'

So Anna was anxious for the future of their business, but Lorna could not credit that Miles would consider that more important than their love.

'I still don't believe you,' she said obstinately.

'You won't see Miles again,' Anna reiterated. 'He'd be afraid he might fall under your spell again.'

'I don't use any spells,' Lorna cried indignantly, while hope raised its head. Anna for her own reasons did not want her to communicate with Miles, but that did not mean that Miles would not contact her. 'I haven't tried to catch him,' she went on, 'if that's what you're implying. Fate threw us together and we fell in love. It's as simple as that.'

Kismet, Miles had said, a fate they were unable to escape.

'Antony lost a kingdom for Cleopatra,' Anna announced. 'That seems a fitting simile in these surroundings, but you're no Cleopatra, my dear. I can't see Miles forgetting honour and other claims for your sake. I tell you, Miles will never come back to you.'

'You certainly don't intend that he should,' Lorna declared bitterly. 'I don't know what he is to you ...?' She looked at Anna questioningly.

'More than my life,' Anna said sincerely. 'Though there's nothing erotic between us. I've no sex allure for men like Miles. I understand him, which you don't, and our friendship will outlast any light loves. I will not permit him to throw himself away upon a silly little girl who is blindly infatuated with him.'

'Thank you, you're not being very polite. I wouldn't do anything to harm Miles, but I've got to be convinced I'm bad for him, which I don't think I am. There's too much of the green-eyed monster about your arguments, Miss Orman, and I'm not afraid of your influence over him.'

But she was, for presumably Anna knew Miles much better than Lorna did after their short tempestuous association. Could she possibly be right about him? She leaned her head against the window pane, which was closed to preserve the air-conditioning. Below her the river that was Egypt's lifeline pursued its long journey to the sea, but there was no metaphoric river to alleviate the aridity of a future without Miles. He had flashed through her life like a comet, filling it with radiance for one brief moment, then sped away into the unknown leaving darkness behind him.

Anna rose to her feet, her face contorted with sudden passion.

'I'd rather see Miles dead than married to you!'

Lorna stared at her aghast. This was the Oriental in Anna coming to the surface, a vindictive, vengeful Anna, whose vehemence shocked her. Then her features became impassive again.

'Young people think the world has come to an end if they are thwarted in their desires, but everything is transitory. Go home, Lorna, and find a nice solid man to care for you. When one door closes another opens, that's life.'

Lorna's whole being surged upwards in violent denial. If a door had closed upon Miles it had also shut upon the love of her life. She could not conceive that she would ever love another man.

'Thank you,' she said coldly, 'but in spite of my looks I'm not fickle. If you see Miles you might tell him that I'll wait, even if it's forever.'

'I shan't mention you to Miles,' Anna retorted. 'He will have forgotten you as you had better forget him. Good day, Miss Travers.'

She went out briskly without waiting for Lorna's rejoinder. Lorna remained motionless by the window. Forgotten, in a week? No, there Anna had over-reached herself. Miles might have second thoughts, might even cruelly repudiate her, but he would not forget her so soon.

She waited through the rest of the week and the one following it, hoping against hope to receive some word from Miles. She could not believe that he would not send one if only to explain why he had not come in person. He could not be so inconsiderate as to leave her in suspense. But no word came. Unwillingly she had to accept that Anna had been his messenger, and the message had been loud and clear. He preferred to stay in Egypt with Anna and he did not want to see her again in case she distracted him from his purpose. He was not worth the sleepless hours and the secret tears which she shed at night. He had said, when he was holding her in his arms, words which he regretted as soon as he had left her.

The bustle of preparations for their departure gave Lorna plenty to do. All Lady Augusta's papers had to be carefully indexed before packing so she would know exactly where to find them upon arrival. The weather reports informed them spring had come to Britain and in Egypt the days became hotter and hotter.

Arrived back in England, Lorna settled down in her aunt's flat, throughout a temperate summer. No message came from Miles and she no longer expected one, for she had made a devastating discovery which seemed to confirm all Anna had said. Wondering if she dare ring up his home to enquire about him, she looked through the telephone directory and found no Favershams were listed in Marlow. Upon consulting a street directory, her search produced the same result. There were no Favershams in Marlow, so what he had told her about his people and his home was a fabrication, though she could see no point in it. Why talk about taking her to a house which did not exist? There was no answer to that, except that everything to do with Miles, including his love, appeared to be phoney.

Lady Augusta was at home twice a week, and Lorna helped at these evening parties by ensuring that everyone was supplied with food and drink and the buffet was kept replenished. The people who came were mostly middle-aged, distinguished politicians, servicemen and civil servants. Occasionally a younger person would put in an appearance, a relative of one of the elders, but they rarely came twice. One who did was Lionel Cartwright, a fresh-faced young man of about twenty-five. He always made straight for Lorna, and after a while summoned up courage to ask her out to a theatre or a concert. He was pleasant and unassuming and Lorna liked him.

His attentions did not escape Lady Augusta's eagle eye, and she said to her niece:

'You've made a hit there, my dear, and you could do a lot worse. He's steady and his family are well-to-do. He would provide for your future which I'm afraid I can't do. I can only leave you a pittance, most of my money is to go to good causes and in any case I don't believe in inherited wealth.'

'I don't expect anything,' Lorna told her with a grateful look. 'I anticipate I'll always be able to earn a living.'

'But you'll be lonely. A family is an anchor. I denounce domestic drudgery, but marriage can be a partnership if both do their share, and you'll find young Lionel easy to manage. Women are happier married, and even a bad marriage is better than none. Spinsters dry up and compensate themselves by making nuisances of themselves, like I do.'

'Oh no, Aunt Augusta,' Lorna protested. 'You do a lot of useful work.' (She had sometimes doubted its value.) 'You'll be terribly missed.'

Augusta smiled wryly. 'Thank you dear, but I'll be more missed than regretted. If Lionel proposes, accept him.'

'I don't love him.'

'But you like him? He isn't physically repulsive to you? That's all that matters. Romantic love is only a marsh light, often leading into bogs.'

Lorna thought over what her aunt had said and admitted its wisdom. She was not naturally an independent character, and she needed someone to lean upon. Probably the liking she had for Lionel would develop into affection, which was so much more stable than the passion she had felt for Miles. They had tastes in common, they enjoyed the same plays and both appreciated classical music. Best of all, he could give her children and in them she would find fulfilment. With a wrench at her heart she recalled Miles' words: 'Only yours.' She could not visualise Miles in a domestic setting—in the desert, yes, or by the statues of Memnon, anywhere wild and strange; there was an untamed element about him that fascinated even while it repelled. But she must not think of Miles. He had disappeared into the blue and the period in Egypt had assumed a dreamlike quality. Sometimes she did dream of huge colonnades and crumbling pillars, beneath which Miles was standing in Arab dress, the fire of passion alight in his eyes, but she could not reach him. That was the nightmare part of the dream. Though he held out his arms some invisible force was restraining her and she woke to an agony of loss. Then as the placid summer days slid past, the dream became rarer until it almost ceased.

Meanwhile there was Lionel with his eyes expressing shy admiration. He was shy, he would not approach her unless she encouraged him, but as yet she had been unable to bring herself to do so.

Summer passed into autumn. The trees in the park turned russet and gold and strewed their largesse over the grass and paths. It was six months since Lorna had returned from Egypt, and she was over the worst of her grief. By carefully avoiding any reminder of what might have been she had reached a stage of placid resignation.

Then one morning her calm was shattered.

She was working in the small room which was used as an office when the telephone rang, and she mechanically picked up the receiver.

'Lady Augusta Clavering's residence.'

'Lorna? It is you, isn't it?'

Lorna's heart seemed to stop and she went rigid, she had never expected to hear that voice again.

'Miles,' she breathed. 'Oh, no!'

'Oh yes. Darling, did I startle you?'

'I'd say you did!' she laughed shakily. 'I . . . I didn't expect . . . Miles, are you all right?'

It had occurred to her more than once that he might have been ill or met with an accident, but during the six months that had elapsed, surely he could have sent at least a postcard to reassure her? She had given him her London address and he had said it was engraved upon his heart. He had also told her that if anything happened to him she would be advised, but no word had come to her so that she had ruled out that possibility.

He laughed in response to her question and replied in his familiar bantering tones:

'I'm quite all right except for a scratch which has rather spoilt my beauty. I got that on the day I meant to return to Cairo. I hope it won't put you off.'

So something had happened, but so long ago it did not account for half a year's silence. She said reproachfully:

'You could have written.'

'It wasn't possible; I was . . . delayed. But I can't tell you about it over the phone. Will you meet me somewhere?'

Her first impulse was to cry yes, yes, anywhere you say, but she checked it. This cool assumption that she was ready to be picked up again after months of wilful neglect seemed to her to be sheer effrontery, and she distrusted his glib tongue. A thought struck her.

'Where are you speaking from?' she asked.

'My home, of course.' He sounded surprised. 'I'm with my people in Marlow.'

'Have they moved recently?'

'Good lord no, they've always been here.'

But they were not there, that she had ascertained. He had told her it was his only permanent address, but it was a fictitious one. She could not begin to understand why he had deceived her about it, was continuing the deceit. Then the remembrance of all the suffering he had caused her submerged her in a wave of fierce resentment, killing the joy she had felt at the sound of his voice.

'Well, darling,' he sounded impatient, 'Where and when? I'm longing to see you.'

He was ignoring the dreary months of separation as if they had never been. She stifled her own longing and said frigidly:

'I'm sorry, Miles, but I'd rather not meet you. You've caused so much havoc in my life that I'm reluctant to start it all up again.'

'But I can explain ...'

'Can you? Listen, you were coming back to me six months ago. Since then I've had no word or sign from you. You say you were delayed—your precious business, I suppose. I ... I can't take any more.'

'There were reasons ...'

'Of course. You'd explain away anything, but I think Anna gave me the real ones for your non-appearance.'

'Anna?' He sounded startled. 'When did you see her?'

'The day before you were due back. She gave me your message.'

'I didn't send any message by Anna.'

'I think you did. She told me you would never come back, that you didn't mean to return and hadn't the courage to tell me so yourself. She implied that I was the biggest catastrophe that had ever happened to you.'

Her anger revived as she recalled Anna's insults.

Miles' voice sounded strange, as he asked: 'You believed her?'

'I didn't at the time, but I've been forced to accept that what she said was true. You didn't come back and it's only now that you've remembered my existence.'

'I counted on your faith, your trust . . .'

'Which it seems were misplaced.'

'What's come over you?' he demanded. 'You don't sound like my Lorna any more.'

'That's your doing—and I'm not your Lorna.' She drew a deep breath. 'That's the last thing I want to be!'

A deliberate untruth. The sound of his voice had awoken her dormant senses. Her whole body was crying out for him, but she refused to listen to its urgency. Her brain was warning her it was a snare. If she were foolish enough to meet him as he had requested she would only let herself in for more heartache. Since he was in England he was possibly looking for diversion and had remembered her address—that of Lorna Travers, who was exciting to kiss and deceive with false promises. Perhaps he had believed what he was saying at the time, until other interests and Anna's persuasions changed his mind. She did not want to become involved with him once more now she had learned to live without him, and since she could no longer trust him, he would only cause her further pain.

There was silence from the other end of the wire, but he had not rung off. Desperately she went on:

'Anna was very frank about your character, Miles, she said you would never settle down, you were quite unstable, or words to that effect. You confirmed her words by not turning up, and the conclusion I drew was final.'

'It wasn't possible to communicate with you,' he told her.

'For the whole of six months?' she asked sarcastically. 'That's a long time to be incommunicado. It isn't good enough, Miles.'

'Lorna, I can't tell you about it over the phone. For God's sake let me see you—I'll call at your home if you won't meet me outside.'

'Oh, please don't come here,' she cried agitatedly. She could not bear a meeting between him and Lady Augusta, which might well chance, since she had never mentioned him to her. She must put an end to their present conversation which was becoming more and more hurtful. She wanted so much to see him, and knew to meet him would be unwise.

'Really there's no need to rake up the past,' she went on forcing herself to speak lightly. 'You and I had an abortive affair, but it's over now. I ...I'd almost forgotten you.' Her brittle laugh sounded horribly false in her own ears. 'In fact I've got another admirer, who I think is about to propose.'

'The devil he is! Lorna, I won't accept that ...'

'I'm afraid you'll have to. Miles, you wouldn't want to spoil my chance of happiness with a steady young man, would you? If you come blundering in he may imagine all sorts of things that didn't happen. Please, if you've any consideration for me at all, you'll keep out of the way.'

There was a longish pause, and Lorna gripped the receiver until her knuckles were white. It was all she could do not to cry out that she would meet him anywhere he wanted, that she loved him still, but he had let her down once, he would do so again.

'That's what you really want me to do?' he asked at last, and his voice sounded strained.

'It would be best. We... we only upset each other. If you're on your own in London, I'm sure you can find some pretty girl to keep you company, they always fall for you.'

'But apparently are very quickly consoled,' he said bitterly. 'All right, Lorna, I get the message. You won't be troubled by me any more.'

For a long time after he had rung off, Lorna sat staring at the phone already regretting what she had done. She had acted sensibly, Miles could only disrupt her life again, but Lionel Cartwright was a poor substitute for him whom she still loved with all her heart. Perhaps she should have given him a chance to explain ... explain what? A six months' absence and silence, after he had proposed to marry her within a few weeks? If something had happened to him he could at least have sent a postcard, as apparently he had not forgotten her address. She knew he had a fatal fascination for her and if she saw him she could not trust herself to resist it. She would be wax in his hands, meekly accepting whatever preposterous story he chose to invent. No, she had done the right thing. He had gone out of her life and it would be idiotic folly to allow him to re-enter it. But one thing his reappearance had decided: she knew now she could never marry Lionel Cartwright.

Two evenings later, Lorna was sitting with Lionel at one of her aunt's 'at homes' discussing the opera they had been to hear the week before. She was wondering if she should refuse any further dates, as it was hardly fair to keep him on a string, but until he declared himself there was nothing between them except friendship, and that she needed to solace her. He was in no way bound to her except by his own wish.

'Hullo, there's Eliot Harvey,' he suddenly exclaimed, as a dapper young man, slightly older than himself, wended his way towards them, carrying his glass in his hand. 'Hi, Eliot, I haven't seen you for an age.'

'Oh, I've been around,' the other man returned vaguely. 'But you've had other distractions.' He smiled admiringly at Lorna. 'Introduce me.'

They exchanged pleasantries and Eliot sat down beside them.

'Do you know the Beresfords?' he asked Lionel.

'Only slightly. I was at school with Chris. Of course I was only a snotty junior and he was Head Boy and a rugger ace. I suppose I hero-worshipped him a bit in the way of small boys. I remember he had the bluest eyes I've ever seen.'

Lorna winced; she did not want to be reminded of blue eyes. Fortunately Lionel's were brown.

'I've often wondered what happened to him,' Lionel went on. 'Didn't he go into the Army?'

'Yes, but he resigned his commission after his first term of duty, much to his parents' disgust, and for the last few years nothing has been heard of him. Now he's home.'

'Really? I'd like to meet him again. What's he been doing?'

The two men seemed to have settled down to talk about this Chris Beresford, who was unknown to Lorna and therefore of no interest to her. She looked around, half inclined to leave them, but there was no one else she knew, and she hoped they would soon find another subject.

'Having a bad time,' Eliot told him. 'I haven't seen him myself, but his father told me—you know we're very friendly with Mr and Mrs Beresford— that he had a most unpleasant experience abroad— got beaten up by some thugs and was left for dead. He was found by an old native boatman—you know Chris always was pally with our brown brothers— who tended him until he was more or less recovered. Hugh Beresford said he was hit about the head resulting in temporary amnesia and his face is scarred. Apparently he's very much the worse for wear.'

Lorna yawned behind her hand. She was sorry for this Chris Beresford, but assault and battery were becoming commonplace nowadays, and he had probably been drunk and insulted somebody. She had much rather talk about opera.

'Where was he, when this happened?' Lionel asked.

'In Upper Egypt.'

Lorna's attention was caught. Upper Egypt had associations for her.

'But what on earth was he doing out there?'

Eliot lowered his head and whispered something.

'Oh, come off it!' Lionel laughed. 'We all know that the classic espionage agent is obsolete. Modern intelligence uses satellites, electronics and aeroplanes.'

'That's military intelligence,' Eliot told him, 'but there's still a need for what's called ecological data, that is information about the activities of the people themselves, especially in these days of communist penetration. Sudden revolutions are all the mode, and can be a threat to British interests. The Government likes to be kept informed of which way the cat is likely to jump. We know Nasser got rid of his communist advisers, but those fellows never give up. They infiltrate everywhere, and what with all this trouble in the rest of Africa, who knows what might be brewing.'

Lorna's interest waned. Politics, she thought; could anything be more dreary? Meanwhile Eliot continued with the Chris Beresford saga.

'He'd been reported missing, so of course his family is jubilant now he's turned up alive—the return of the prodigal son isn't in it. Especially as I understand he's retired and going to take up something a bit more conventional. Of course he wouldn't be in the state he is if he could have had proper nursing, but he had to lie low, and it took him nearly six months to get on his feet again.

Eventually the British Embassy was able to smuggle him out.'

Six months was a period that had a significance for Lorna, and her hands clenched on her lap as a sudden suspicion began to grow. The old boatman on the Nile with whom Miles had seemed so friendly, the 'scratch' he had mentioned, the long silence since he had gone to Upper Egypt, which Eliot's story explained.

'There's a tale being told,' Eliot went on; both men seemed to be fascinated by the exploits of Chris Beresford, 'that he used a most original cover-up, getting himself hired as an extra by a film company on location in the desert, but that I don't believe ... Miss Travers, are you all right?'

Lorna stared at him blankly, while all the little things which had puzzled her began to click into place. Chris Beresford ... Miles Faversham ... naturally he would not have been using his own name, and that was why she had been unable to find it in the telephone directory, but if he were, and what Eliot was relating was what had happened to him, what had she done? Oh God, how could she have said those cruel things to him?

With an immense effort she pulled herself together and rose to her feet.

'Oh, I'm all right. It's a bit hot in here ... if you'll excuse me ...' She took an uncertain step, intent only upon escape. Incidents which had little significance at the time were crowding into her memory, and she recalled that he had once told her: 'I'm giving up everything for you,' which she had not understood. While she had deplored his seemingly aimless way of life he had been serving his country in the manner in which his peculiar talents were suited.

Now Lionel began to fuss, alarmed by her white face.

'Can I get you anything? Do you feel faint? Shall I call Lady Augusta?'

'Oh no, no, please. You stay with your friend. I'll get some aspirin and lie down for a while.' Somehow she managed to get away from him and out of the crowded room, her head in a whirl.

Alone in her room, Lorna sank down upon her bed, clasping her aching head. Of course Miles could not tell her what he was really doing, but he had asked her to trust him and she had not done so. Her great love had failed at the first test. She had plenty of excuses—his evasiveness, the shortness of their association, the poison Anna had poured into her ears, but she should have gone to him when he had phoned her. He had told her he would come to her in the end, 'though hell should bar the way', in the words of Alfred Noyes' poem. He had been through hell and come, and what had she done? Refused to see him, put him off with a silly fairy tale about Lionel Cartwright ... what must he be thinking of her?

But he was at home in England now, and she could phone him, no difficulty about the number now she knew his real name. She would abase herself, figuratively crawl to his feet, do anything to make amends, and if he still loved her he would forgive.

The telephone was in the office, but that on these occasions, was used as an ante-room and visitors continually went in and out. But Lady Augusta had an extension in her bedroom, and thither Lorna went. The number was listed under Beresford,—The Lilacs, Marlow. With fast beating heart she dialled it, praying that Miles himself would answer it. But it was a strange man's voice who replied.

'Is M ... C ... Chris there?' she asked, stumbling over the unfamiliar name.

There was a pause and the voice asked who was speaking.

'Lorna Travers. I ... I'm a friend of his. I've just heard he's back. Can I speak to him?'

There was a pause, and then Chris's father told her:

'I'm sorry, but that's not possible. My son has not been well and he has gone away to a quiet place to recuperate. His friends can help him best by leaving him alone.'

'But ...' With a pang she recalled how Miles had teased her about her constant use of the word. 'It's very important that I contact him, Mr Beresford. Couldn't you tell me where he is and then I could phone or write.'

The voice that answered her was horribly facetious.

'My dear young lady, I'm sure you've better things to do than run after Chris. He's not in a fit state to escort you anywhere, or appreciate female friends.'

'I ... I'm ... I mean ...' she was becoming incoherent.

Mr Beresford's voice became very cold. 'My dear, you sound almost hysterical. Emotional girls are the last thing he wants to see. Forgive me for being blunt. If he had wanted to communicate with you he would have told us, but he insisted he wanted to be let alone.'

He rang off.

Her guests departed, Lady Augusta came into her room, wondering where her niece had gone. She found her slumped beside the telephone crying as if her heart would break.

CHAPTER TEN

LADY AUGUSTA was fond of her niece and had always believed she was a sensible, level-headed sort of girl. This terrible, desperate weeping shocked and amazed her. She had never before seen Lorna cry. Some long-buried maternal instinct stirred within her and she gathered the girl into her arms, uttering soothing noises, and begging her to desist.

Lorna threw her arms about her scrawny neck, clinging to her as if she were the mother she had lost, and gradually her weeping ceased.

'Tell me about it,' Lady Augusta bade her. 'It helps to talk. I'm not blind and I saw something was wrong, but I don't believe in forcing confidences and I thought you had got over it.'

Bit by bit, at first disjointedly but more coherently as she went on, Lorna poured out the whole story and felt the better for the telling of it.

Her aunt was astonished that her quiet, reserved niece was capable of such intense emotion, but characteristically what interested her was Miles' activities.

'Here, wipe your eyes,' she said, giving Lorna a clean handkerchief. 'Nothing's so bad that it can't be remedied.' She stroked Lorna's silky head with unwonted tenderness, but her mind was elsewhere.

'Chris Beresford,' she went on musingly. 'I met him once when he was in the Army. Good-looking lad with a way with him. I'm not surprised you fell for him. I did hear he was attached to the Embassy in Cairo, but I never ran across him while I was in Egypt.'

'He took care of that,' Lorna told her, reminded of the various occasions upon which Miles had refused to meet her aunt. 'He'd be afraid you'd recognise him since he was supposed to be somebody else.' She wrinkled her fine brows. 'How could he be attached to that?'

'Why not?' Lady Augusta chuckled. 'He had to be attached to something, and all the Embassy staff are Intelligence agents of one sort or another, from the Ambassador downwards, though in the higher echelons they call it diplomacy. You'd be surprised at the amount of information that's gathered from overseas from all sources, including the embassies. Data on trade, finance, natural resources, industrial capacity, even the personal characteristics of national decision-makers, anything that indicates the capabilities and intentions of foreign nations. It's not all undercover work, of course, and a lot of it is extraneous matter, which the S.I.S. at home have to tabulate and sort out for anything signficant. Intelligence is a most fascinating subject and has a great appeal for the general public, judging by the quantity of inaccurate fiction published about it.'

During this long discourse, Lorna had recovered her self-possession, which was why Lady Augusta had delivered it. She saw with relief that her niece was herself again. But Lorna was not in the least interested in Intelligence as a subject, only as it affected Miles.

'What do you suppose Miles ... I mean Chris ... was looking for?' she asked.

'Only he can tell you that, and of course he never will,' Lady Augusta told her drily. 'If he had been sent out into the field it was because some high-up needed some special information. I was always suspicious myself about the goings on of that old sinner Ibrahim at Sidi Dara, but I don't know whose side he was on. That's why I wanted to meet him. I wonder if your appearance in the desert assisted his cover-up or whether you were an embarrassment to him.'

'An embarrassment, I should think,' Lorna said bitterly. 'I've always been that to him.'

'In fiction there's usually a beautiful woman mixed up in it, though often she's a double agent.'

Anna! Anna Orman was not beautiful, but she was mixed up in it. Miles had been working with her and she had fiercely resented Lorna's intervention. Now the veil which had hung over Miles' activities had been lifted, she realised how many difficulties she must have presented. He had fallen in love with her and she had been an impediment in the work he had been ordered to do.

'I suppose he had nearly completed his assignment and he meant to bring you home, marry you and resign,' Lady Augusta said thoughtfully. 'It was hard luck he got set upon on the very day he was due back. Almost looks as if someone knew and wanted to prevent him.'

Lorna had a mental vision of a dark vindictive face and Anna's words returned to her. 'I'd rather see Miles dead than married to you.' But no, Anna loved him, she wouldn't, couldn't engineer anything so dreadful.

'You don't mind, what he was doing?' her aunt enquired.

'No, why should I?' Lorna cried passionately. 'I don't care what he was, is, or will be, I'll always love him. He was always decent and kind to me.' She recalled his ministrations in the tent when he must have been wishing her elsewhere. 'But when he came back, and he'd been terribly ill, that Eliot man said, I wouldn't listen to him. My stupid pride and rancour at his supposed desertion took possession of me. I even told him Lionel had superseded him!'

. 'Lionel might be a better proposition,' Lady Augusta suggested slyly. 'He's younger and ... er ... less hardbitten.'

'Don't talk like that!' Lorna flared. 'It's Miles or nobody, but I've abused his faith and trust and I'll never forgive myself.'

'I believe you really do love him,' Lady Augusta said wonderingly. 'True love is rare, and I don't see how he can blame you too hardly. Six months is a long time, and how were you to guess he was laid up in some waterman's hovel with a hole in his head? It's a most unusual thing to happen, and most girls would have forgotten him.'

'That's what he thinks I've done, and I wouldn't listen to him.'

'Oh yes, you told me that.' And, as Lorna threatened to weep again: 'Now pull yourself together and let us consider what's to be done.'

'He's gone away,' Lorna wailed. 'His father

wouldn't tell me where, and said he didn't want to see anyone.'

'Oh, I'll find out; if Hugh Beresford won't tell me, there are other sources. I'm not a bad sleuth myself when I get going.'

'But suppose he doesn't want to see me?'

'Of course he will.' Lady Augusta's hard face suddenly softened, and a dreamy look came into her eyes. 'I believe, and it's an odd thing for an old warhorse like myself to admit, that there are people who are the two parts of one whole. This Chris–Miles, whatever he calls himself, can no more resist you than you can withstand him. Once you meet, all will be well.'

'Oh, Aunt Augusta!' Lorna stared at her aunt in surprise. Such words from the cynical supporter of women's rights was most unexpected.

'It was not my fate to meet my other half,' the elder woman went on. 'Many of us don't, and as I would not accept anything less, I stayed single.'

'That's why I couldn't marry Lionel,' Lorna told her.

'Poor Lionel, he'll get over it and perhaps find his true mate. Now you'd better go to bed. Promise me you won't cry any more.'

Lorna didn't, but she lay awake for a long time going over the events in Egypt in the light of her new knowledge. Certainly it seemed as if she and Miles had been drawn together by an irresistible force. He had fought against it, not wanting to succumb, but in the end it had conquered him on the night he had proposed. She hoped and prayed it would work again when at last they met.

Two days later, Augusta handed Lorna a slip of

paper on which was written an address in Tintagel, Cornwall, with a triumphant smile.

'You can borrow the car,' she told her. 'I don't use it much in town. The weather is clear, so you should make it in a day.' Her smile broadened mischievously. 'I'll expect you back when I see you.'

Lorna arrived in Tintagel the following afternoon. The crowds of holiday visitors were all gone and the country looked bare and a little desolate, under a grey sky. She knew she would have no difficulty finding accommodation for the night since it was out of season, but what would have happened by nightfall?

She found the street and the homely-looking boarding house where Miles was apparently staying. She parked the car in front of it and with fast beating heart rang the bell.

A motherly-looking woman opened it and looked at her dubiously when she asked for Mr Beresford. The name still seemed strange on her tongue, but she supposed she would become used to it.

'He's out,' she was told. 'He does a lot of walking. Was he expecting you, miss? He told me I was to turn away any visitors.'

'He *is* expecting me,' Lorna lied. 'I've driven all the way from London to bring him an important message.' Which was in a way true. 'Can you tell me which way he usually goes?'

If she could not find him, she would sit all night on the doorstep sooner than be baulked now.

The woman hesitated, but something in Lorna's wistful face decided her. The steady gaze of her wide grey eyes was honest and appealing. No brassy tart this, pursuing a reluctant boyfriend, but, as she put it later to her husband, 'a sweetly pretty young lady.' She had perhaps come to clear up a misunderstanding, for she had suspected that her lodger had some grave trouble from his brooding sadness and the lost look in his eyes. Being of a romantic turn of mind, she had decided it must be a love affair.

'He usually goes down to the castle,' she told Lorna. 'It's his favourite haunt, though it's a mite gloomy this weather. Mind how you go, because if he's up there the climb can be treacherous this time of year.'

Lorna thanked her and got into the car.

She drove slowly down the rough road which led to the castle. On either side of her were rocky tors with ragged bunches of heather clinging to their crevices, and jackdaws circling round them. It ended in an open space where cars could be parked. Getting out of it, Lorna looked about her.

Ahead of her was the great mass of rock on the summit of which the remains of the castle were situated. The castle where tradition said Uther and Igraine had plighted their troth, the parents of Arthur.

The result of that illicit union had been war and strife, and her surroundings were a fitting scene for dark deeds. The forbidding castle was approached by ladder-like steps after crossing a plank bridge under which water was swirling, agitated by the breeze which was blowing. To her left was another high tor, with the broken walls of old fortifications on its crest. To her right was a path strewn with boulders and stones which led down to a beach in front of a series of caves. Which way had Miles gone? She looked apprehensively up at the castle. It would be a stiff climb and the wind at the top would be unpleasant. She shivered in spite of her suede jacket, for the breeze was stiffening, and drew its fur collar up about her neck. The scene was wild and grim and the screaming gulls added to its desolation.

Then she noticed on the far side of the little bay into which the water under the bridge was streaming a strip of gravelly sand, and standing upon it a solitary figure in a dark leather jacket, hands in pockets and shoulders hunched against the wind, gazing out to sea. It was Miles, and her heart seemed to turn over. She ran to the top of the rough steps which gave access to the beach, calling his name. The wind carried her voice away, but he must have sensed her presence, for he turned round and saw her poised above the steps, her fair hair streaming out behind her like a flag.

As he came towards her she saw he was much thinner, his clothes seemed to hang upon him, and his face was pale and drawn. There was an only recently healed scar down one side of his face from temple to jawline. Her heart contracted at this evidence of suffering.

She stumbled down the steps as he reached them, missed the bottom ones and fell headlong into his arms.

'Oh, Miles, Miles,' she sobbed, reiterating his name over and over again. Then she remembered he was not called Miles. 'I'll never be able to call you Chris.'

'You needn't. Miles is my middle name—Christian Miles Beresford.'

He knew from what she had said that she had learned the truth, but explanations, apologies, atonement and forgiveness were not necessary in that moment of reunion. They had found each other again, and that was all that mattered.

Back at Miles' lodging, seated before a blazing fire in his private sitting room, warmth and happiness brought colour into Miles' face, making the red scar less noticeable, and nothing could dim the vivid blue of his eyes. There were, however, grey hairs among the brown as Lorna noticed with a sigh, re-calling the day at Mena House when Patricia had searched and found none.

She sat on the rug at his feet her head against his knees, and his fingers strayed through her soft hair. She had discarded her jacket and the white sweater she wore moulded the delicate curves of her figure.

Suddenly she asked:

'Do you know what happened to Anna?'

'She's dead,' he said shortly. 'Killed in a car crash in Cairo.'

He expressed no regret and Lorna wondered if he suspected the same thing which she had done. So Anna was gone and her sins were buried with her. Her soul would be weighed in the balance by Anubis—or a Greater One—and it was not for them to judge her. Lorna knew that her name would never be mentioned by either of them again.

Miles sighed and moved in his chair. Putting his hands beneath Lorna's arms, he lifted her on to his knees. Holding her close, he murmured:

'If only you knew how often I've dreamed of this!

You and I alone before an open fire. We must have a real fireplace in our home, Lorna—none of your all-electric.'

Our home. Two wonderful words, but a little doubt lingered; would Miles be content to stay put?

'You won't want to wander any more?' she asked anxiously.

'No, and I'll tell you something.' He drew her a little closer. 'All my life I've been searching for something, I didn't know what. I've undertaken dangerous assignments in strange places, and still this inexplicable urge drove me on, but now my quest is ended.'

'Where did you find what you were looking for?' she queried.

'Beside the Nile. Don't you understand? I believe it was you, my darling. I found you only to lose you, but now we're together I'm at rest.'

Perhaps there was something in Lady Augusta's theory after all, Lorna thought, but it was amazing that two such tough and hardbitten people should harbour such a sentimental idea.

'You're more romantic than I am,' she told him.

'And what's wrong with romance? God knows we need something to brighten the sombre times in which we live.' He laid his cheek against hers. 'Never leave me, darling.'

'I think it would kill me to leave you now,' she said earnestly.

His mouth closed over hers and they clung together in silent rapture, while the fire turned red and glowing and the autumn dusk closed in on them.

Titles available this month in the
Mills & Boon ROMANCE Series

SENTIMENTAL JOURNEY *by Janet Dailey*
Jessica found no difficulty at all in responding to Brodie Hayes's devastating attraction – but could she ever be anything but a substitute for her beautiful sister Jordanna?

TEMPTED BY DESIRE *by Carole Mortimer*
Vidal Martino was the man of Suzanne's dreams – so why couldn't her bitchy stepmother transfer her attention away from Vidal to his even richer brother Cesare?

CLOSE TO THE HEART *by Rebecca Stratton*
Lisa had crossed swords with the formidable Yusuf ben Dacra – but he had turned the tables on her and now she was completely in his power.

CASTLE OF THE FOUNTAINS *by Margaret Rome*
Visiting Sicily, Rosalba discovered that the old custom of vendetta was by no means dead – not as long as Salvatore Diavolo had anything to do with it!

THE SHEIK'S CAPTIVE *by Violet Winspear*
'If you save a life, you own it,' the Sheik Khasim ben Haran had told Diane – and he had saved her from the heat of the desert . . .

THE VITAL SPARK *by Angela Carson*
It was obvious to Lee that Haydn Scott intended to take over her family business – was he going to take her over as well?

MOONLIGHT ON THE NILE *by Elizabeth Ashton*
Working in Egypt, Lorna had fallen in love with the mysterious Miles Faversham. But was she right to trust her heart and her whole future to him?

POSSESSION *by Charlotte Lamb*
Laura was horribly afraid that Dan Harland didn't just want possession of the family firm; he wanted her too . . .

PACT WITHOUT DESIRE *by Jane Arbor*
Sara had rashly accepted Rede Forrest's proposal of marriage, and she hadn't anticipated all the emotional problems what would arise . . .

THE JADE GIRL *by Daphne Clair*
What was it about Alex Lines that made Stacy so resentful when he came to live in her home for a few weeks?

Mills & Boon Romances
– all that's pleasurable in Romantic Reading!

Available August 1979

Forthcoming Mills & Boon Romances

RETURN TO DEVIL'S VIEW by *Rosemary Carter*
Jana could only succeed in her search for some vital information by working as secretary to the enigmatic Clint Dubois — and it was clear that Clint suspected her motives . . .

THE MAN ON THE PEAK by *Katrina Britt*
The last thing Suzanne had wanted or expected when she went to Hong Kong for a holiday was to run into her ex-husband Raoul . . .

TOGETHER AGAIN by *Flora Kidd*
Ellen and Dermid Craig had separated, but now circumstances had brought Ellen back to confront Dermid again. Was this her chance to rebuild her marriage, or was it too late?

A ROSE FROM LUCIFER by *Anne Hampson*
Colette had always loved the imposing Greek Luke Marlis, but only now was he showing that he was interested in her. Interested — but not, it seemed, enough to want to marry her . . .

THE JUDAS TRAP by *Anne Mather*
When Sara Fortune fell in love with Michael Tregower, and he with her, all could have ended happily. Had it not been for the secret that Sara dared not tell him . . .

THE TEMPESTUOUS FLAME by *Carole Mortimer*
Caroline had no intention of marrying Greg Fortnum, whom she didn't even know apart from his dubious reputation — so she escaped to Cumbria where she met the mysterious André . . .

WITH THIS RING by *Mary Wibberley*
Siana had no memory of who she really was. But what were Matthew Craven's motives when he appeared and announced that he was going to help her find herself again?

SOLITAIRE by *Sara Craven*
The sooner Marty got away from Luc Dumarais the better, for Luc was right out of her league, and to let him become important to her would mean nothing but disaster . . .

SWEET COMPULSION by *Victoria Woolf*
Marcy Campion was convinced that she was right not to let Randal Saxton develop her plot of land — if only she could be equally convinced about her true feelings for Randal!

SHADOW OF THE PAST by *Robyn Donald*
Morag would have enjoyed going back to Wharuaroa, where she had been happy as a teenager, if it hadn't meant coming into constant contact with Thorpe Cunningham.

Available September 1979

191

192